ALSO BY YOEL HOFFMANN
Available from New Directions

Katschen & The Book of Joseph

כרנהרד

Bernhard

אי'נו
הופמ

YOEL HOFFMANN

Translated by Alan Treister

WITH EDDIE LEVENSTON

NEW DIRECTIONS

Bernhard is published by arrangement with the Harris/Elon Agency and the Keter Publishing Company of Israel.

Design by Semadar Megged
First published clothbound in 1998
Manufactured in the United States of America.
New Directions Books are printed on acid-free paper.
Published simultaneously in Canada by Penguin Books
Canada Limited.

Library of Congress Cataloging-in-Publication Data:

Hoffmann, Yoel.
      [Bernhart. English]
      Bernhard / Yoel Hoffmann ; translated by Alan Treister
      with Eddie Levenston.
          p.   cm.
      ISBN 0-8112-1389-7 (alk. paper)
      I. Treister, Alan.   II. Title.
      PJ5054.H6319B4713   1998
      892.4'36—dc21   98-25231
                                                              CIP

New Directions Books are published for James Laughlin
by New Directions Publishing Corporation
80 Eighth Avenue, New York 10011

Bernhard

Prologue*

When a baby is born, someone records the birth. That's how the names of all the children (apart from those born in a street or a field) get registered. Sometimes there's a mistake and they register, for instance, "Britz" instead of "Fritz." And sometimes a man says his name is "Fritz," but no one believes him. Anyway, before Bernhard was born he was wrapped in thin skin in the belly of his mother Clara, as if in a pocket. He moved up and down, and Clara said, "The baby is moving" (she didn't yet know his name would be "Bernhard"). You mustn't be too clever in that kind of thing. Bernhard's organs slowly took shape (he wasn't formed all at once) until he became a complete baby. Moreover inside him there was another baby and inside that baby yet another, and so on ad infinitum. But when people (who act through force of habit) saw that Gustav too was shaped like a baby, they assumed he was a baby. That's why when Gustav crawled on the wooden floor no one wondered why he (that is, Gustav) was so close to the earth's crust.

*This page appears on the back cover of the book in the Hebrew edition.

1

AFTER HIS WIFE DIED, BERNHARD THOUGHT: "The world is infinite. Beyond every galaxy there's another galaxy." He tried to imagine how Paula, her flesh pale, was gradually becoming one with the vast order of the Universe. But Paula's death was not such a simple matter. "Where," thought Bernhard to himself, "is Paula now?"

When Bernhard was born

WHEN BERNHARD WAS BORN EVERYONE said "Sigmund and Clara have had a baby." Some said: "They've had a baby, Sigmund and Clara" and a few said "Clara and Sigmund have had a baby" or "They've had a baby, Clara and Sigmund." What can be told about Bernhard's childhood? Most of the time Bernhard played with a lump of wax (in due course he came to Palestine by himself). Once, in the "Black Forest," a little girl called Lotte said to Bernhard: "Und wie heisst du?"* and Bernhard said: "Bernhard Stein." For a moment, it seemed then to Bernhard (they had dressed him in leather shorts called knickerbockers) that everything would happen of its own accord.

In spite of being a widower

*And what's your name? (German)

3

IN SPITE OF BEING A WIDOWER, BERNHARD
is a work of art. No one can make a Bernhard. At
times, Bernhard himself is seized with wonder.
How, he asks himself, from a speck of matter the
size of a mustard seed have I become what I am (a
complex unique creature)? Once Bernhard read in a
book by Descartes that in the human body, in that
part which is called the pineal gland, there is a soul,
and that is why man is infinitely superior to the rest
of creation, inferior only to God. And God exists,
since God is the most perfect being, and what is absolutely perfect lacks nothing, not a single one of the
qualities found in the world. And one of the qualities found in the world is existence (this is the
quality which distinguishes between what exists
and what does not exist. For example, between a
picture of a stove and a stove). Hence, if God does
not exist, He cannot be absolutely perfect, since
perfection is more perfect if it exists than if it does
not exist. Hence absolute perfection cannot fail to
exist and hence (wrote Descartes) God exists. But
when Bernhard and Paula moved from the German
Colony to Strauss Street, the book by Descartes got
lost.

The house on Strauss Street

THE HOUSE ON STRAUSS STREET, BENBENISHTI says, belongs to the deceased woman's sister (he thinks all women are full-bodied, thinks Bernhard), but "personal belongings, sir, you are entitled to remove." Lately the veins in his legs have become swollen, so he is going to travel, Benbenishti says, on doctor's orders to Beirut. The Lord, he says, will console Bernhard with the rest of the mourners of Zion and Jerusalem. Bernhard thinks: "If El Greco had not painted *The Agony in the Garden of Gethesemane*, the veins in Benbenishti's legs would not be swollen. And conversely, if the veins in Benbenishti's legs had not become swollen, El Greco would not have painted *The Agony in the Garden of Gethesemane*. Man distinguishes one thing from another because of his shortsightedness. But in the eyes of God—who does not have to wait for events to happen but sees all three dimensions of time at once—all things are but one, simple thing." He locks up the house on Strauss Street (Paula's straw hats are lying side by side in the darkened hall) and rents a room with a bed and a sink in Prophets Street.

In Prophets Street he thinks

5

IN PROPHETS STREET HE THINKS ABOUT
Paula's first night in the ground (Paula slid into the
grave as though she were longing to get in). He has
an erection. All my life, thinks Bernhard, I shall
dedicate to the search for truth. Finally he composes
a kind of elegy (but doesn't bother to write it down):

(I imagined how)

(I IMAGINED HOW) BERNHARD
Tied a chicken to a metal bar
(A kind of blacksmith's anvil)
And sat by it all his days

> Schlaf, Bernhardlein
> Schliesse deine Äugelein*

*Sleep little Bern-
hard / Close your
tiny eyes (German).*

At night he took the anvil
In one hand (in the other
A chair) and went
Indoors

> Schlaf, Bernhardlein . . .

After he died, the neighbors
Cut the string
With which he tied the leg
(Of the chicken) to the metal bar

> Schlaf, Bernhardlein . . .

But (so I imagined)
The chicken remained, of its own free will,
Five more days
By the house on Strauss Street

> When Bernhard opens his eyes

7

WHEN BERNHARD OPENS HIS EYES AND sees a strange ceiling, he remembers Paula's death. Because of the daylight it seems to him for a moment that Paula is where she ought to be. But when he sees her in his mind's eye (he thinks "Earth fills her mouth"), his heart is fit to break. He looks at his face in the mirror and thinks: "Everything happens but once. And this moment too (Paula dead and Bernhard, in his pajamas, on Prophets Street) will not come again." He tries to picture to himself a world without Bernhard, but always finds himself hiding near the edge of the picture. Visions of the world, Bernhard thinks, are only visions in my mind.

In the café Bernhard sits

IN THE CAFÉ BERNHARD SITS AT A TABLE, half in and half out of doors. He is thinking about the shoe salesman, Herr Saft, who stands in the doorway of his shop on Strauss Street every day and looks at the shoes of the passersby. Herr Saft's voice is hollow, as if something is wrong with his throat. Herr Saft, Bernhard thinks, won't see Paula's shoes any more (clods of earth struck her stomach). He imagines to himself that he too is dead. (Bernhard's body is lying in Ussishkin Square. Moskovitch shouts, "Give him artificial respiration.") Herzog passes by. And though Bernhard cannot remember what happened between him and Herzog, he feels that rather than Herzog owing him, he owes Herzog. His thoughts revolve around the philosophy of Spinoza: Man sees only the external causes, and so is certain that things actually happen. But in truth, the café and Ussishkin Square and all the other sense impressions (colors and forms and sounds and smells) are abstract forms of logic. But this is divine logic, unattainable by man with his narrow spirit.

Gustav Benjamin says

9

GUSTAV BENJAMIN SAYS: "I HEARD WHAT happened (Bernhard thinks: "What happened?")." Gustav takes Bernhard's hand and holds it between his palms. Suddenly Bernhard realizes that his grief at Paula's death is destined to pass. He orders coffee with cream and two rolls. And as he crunches, he repeats to himself (perhaps twenty times): "Es war einmal und ist nicht mehr / ein riesengrosser Teddybär / er war so gross wie ein halbes Brot / und als er starb, da war er tot."* He slowly sips his coffee (thinking: "I've never seen a two-humped camel"), and finally says: "So, Gustav, what's new?"

In the divine plan

*There was once, and is no more / A most enormous teddy bear / As big as half a loaf of bread / And when he died, then was he dead. (German)

IN THE DIVINE PLAN IT HAS RIGHTLY BEEN
decreed that Gustav's arms should reach his knees
(though Gustav, who has free will, may shorten his
arms if he wishes). Gustav speaks well of someone
in whose house he installed a toilet, and praises the
toilet he installed (he has adjusted to Palestine. He
doesn't say "Installator," but rather "plumper")
and Bernhard also is pleased to talk about the toilet
that Gustav installed, and all the rest. Suddenly
Bernhard is filled with joy (he thinks: "Why not?
Why not? Why not?").

    Bernhard's an enormous bird
    (He'll take some luggage) and he'll fly
    To distant lands, people will look
    Up at the sky and then they'll say:
    Look. There's a Bernhard.
    A colorful, enormous bird.
    He is passing through, he's on his way
    To distant lands. His body's light
    He carries all his fifty years
    (Summer, Winter, Spring, and Fall)
    And he loves (or so it seems
    In the café on Ussishkin Square)
    Gustav, and he loves them all.

                    Shining rainbows of light

11

Shining rainbows of light appear in the region of the North Pole (but there is no connection between this phenomenon and the story of Bernhard). Bernhard thinks: "Silvia, gib mit wasser"* and he has no idea why (there are, he thinks, names and sights . . .). Before Paula had died, Bernhard had already thought "Silvia, gib mit wasser." Now that she is gone (in happy times she would call him "Muschl"), the words have as it were detached themselves from the bottom of his soul, risen, and spread throughout his body like a wild growth. Sometimes Bernhard presses a finger against his temple and counts his heartbeats (he thinks, "I'm Bernhard"). At times he thinks "Zeppelin"—the airship named after the German Count von Zeppelin, or "Rabe"—which in English is "crow" or "raven." These thoughts seem to Bernhard very, very odd. "What does it matter," he thinks, "if Charles the Great was the son of Pepin the Short (or perhaps he was his father?)" Bernhard sees that dogs just run about. He derides himself: "And you, you inflated old windbag, what are you," he thinks, "when you've got nothing on?" The words "und so weiter" fascinate him. If Paula had brought a child into the world, the baby would have had another, which in its turn, would have had yet another, and so on. In his mind's eye, Bernhard sees the wheel come full circle and he, Bernhard, holds his dead father Sigmund in his arms and rocks him as his father Sigmund did for him (except that the baby Sigmund's face is wrinkled).

*Sylvia, bring me some water. (German)

To all appearances Bernhard is worthless

TO ALL APPEARANCES BERNHARD IS WORTHLESS (but actually, as the butcher says, he's "aza min git shtikl flaysh az es makht nisht oys vi men shnayt").* On Prophets Street he feels the absence of Paula. A thin line of excrement sticks to his underpants (all he brought with him from the house on Strauss Street was a picture album and some sheets). In the morning he says two or three times: "Ach, mein lieber Gott."† His head is full of lewd visions. He repeats to himself "Ya" and "Nein" until one gets the upper hand. In the café they serve him coffee with cream and two rolls without his asking. He thinks: "Before long I shall become like a character in a so-called realistic story." His soul is tied to Gustav's (he alone knows that Gustav can go beyond his simplicity). He (i.e., Gustav) makes tea for himself and Bernhard. Until the water boils, he (Gustav) stands on his feet and so does Bernhard (Bernhard stands on his own feet). Gustav's kitchen is the kernel of the world, and when Bernhard sees Gustav's electric bulb, he begins to cry.

In December, Bernhard catches a chill

*A piece of meat so fine that it doesn't matter where you slice it. (Yiddish)

†Oh, good god. (German)

13

IN DECEMBER, BERNHARD CATCHES A CHILL
(a deep cold penetrates his body). He goes to the
house on Strauss Street (Bernhard is on the surface
of the world, and doesn't slip off it but when someone reads all this, the planet Earth will be somewhere else entirely, in the darkness) and brings a
kerosene heater but cannot get it to light. His throat
is sore and his cheeks are burning. The doctor orders him to go somewhere else and have his lungs
photographed, and Bernhard goes there and sits on
a bench and hums to himself: "meine Lunge."*   *My lungs
until a clerk, enclosed in a kind of cube, says   (German)
"Stein." For the first time since Paula's death a
woman's fingers touch Bernhard's flesh. The
woman orders him to press his nipples against an
iron plate: "Breathe," she says, "and wait." Bernhard breathes and waits. Afterwards, he sits on the
bench again until the clerk in the cube says: "Stein."

And when Bernhard regains his strength

AND WHEN BERNHARD REGAINS HIS STRENGTH (the photograph showed that he had once been sick with tuberculosis, but the tissues had healed by themselves) he visits Gustav again (who had visited him when he was sick) and there at Gustav's he half says, half doesn't say (the radio is talking about Hitler): "Wer ist Silvia?"* And only because Gustav says: "Silvia?" does Bernhard know that he really said what he said. Afterwards, Bernhard keeps quiet (at times he has trouble passing water—he is forced to press his lower stomach) and Gustav also keeps quiet and the words "Wer ist Silvia" remain (suspended) around the electric bulb.

*Who is Sylvia? (German)

The days are interconnected

THE DAYS ARE INTERCONNECTED LIKE cogwheels. One day rolls into the next. And in Bernhard's body there are bones, and he carries these bones around, every day of his life, by his own strength alone. Once Benbenishti the notary was also a baby. He lay (his skin red) in a cradle decorated with lace. No one imagined the day would come when there would emerge from his throat (two voiceless pharyngeals) the Hebrew for "the sister of the deceased." In Palestine the air is transparent most of the time. No one gives a thought about Bernhard's bones. Benbenishti says (his childhood is sadder than Bernhard's old age): "The deceased did not own any property, but she does have some stocks. These stocks are now in your possession, sir." As he leaves, Bernhard puts his hand behind him and spreads his buttocks.

At times Bernhard and Gustav talk

At times Bernhard and Gustav talk about miracles. Gustav says: "Yesterday an Arab from Jericho brought Doctor Sussman a chicken that had just been hatched and it had four legs." "What of it?" Bernhard says: "Have you ever given any thought to the fact that Hungarian women also give birth?" "And, last year," Gustav says, "at a wedding celebration in Damascus, seventeen people died of fireworks." And Bernhard says: "A man called Feingold is walking, carrying a suitcase."

And, because Hitler invades Poland,

17

AND, BECAUSE HITLER INVADES POLAND,
Gustav stretches strips of sticky paper over the
kitchen windows, which he covers with lengths of
black cloth. He says: "It is not going to end well."
The stocks that Paula left have also lost a great deal
of their value, but this doesn't dampen Bernhard's
spirit. He stares at Gustav under the electric bulb
(whose light is now completely indoors) and thinks
to himself: "Here's good old Gustav." And when
the air is not transparent he goes out into the street
and walks about among the houses (he imagines to
himself that he's a ship). His legs are immersed in
water and his head inhabits a fog. He has no needs
and no possessions. He is an infinite Bernhard. People
pass him by as if in a looking glass.

But, when he returns to Prophets Street,

BUT, WHEN HE RETURNS TO PROPHETS STREET,
he rummages in his pockets and cannot find the key
to the iron gate. He stands and knocks, and waits for
someone to come from inside the house and open
the gate. He lifts his gaze and calls out in a voice nei-
ther loud nor soft. "Hello . . ." Then he knocks
again at the iron gate, but still no one comes from
inside. He lifts his gaze and calls out in a voice
louder than at first, but not really loud: "Hello . . ."
And since no one comes, Bernhard stands there
pondering whether he should raise his voice even
more. Finally he goes over to Gustav's, knocks on
the door and says: "Ich habe meinen Schlüssel ver-
loren."*

*_I've lost my key._
(_German_)

It seems to Bernhard

19

It seems to Bernhard that people are always saying, "Bernhard, pull yourself together" (or "Pull yourself together, Bernhard"). He realizes that he should learn to talk about Borochov* and dance until sweat drips from his armpits, but he doesn't know how to do it. When he came to Palestine (because of the emptiness within) he saw a camel bearing the sun's disc on its back. Then the sun's disc slipped and hung from the camel's underbelly. And at twilight the camel's shadow stood between the end of the sea and the beginning of the sky. From that day on Bernhard looks into the faces of camels that happen to cross his path, and the camels (their eyes say: "Yes, that's the way things are") look into Bernhard's face. At times Bernhard sees himself, in his mind's eye, as Bernhard-the-Camel, with camels all around. And the camels have their feet in the sand on the seashore, and their heads (they graze on stars) in the sky.

*(1881–1919)
Theoretician of
Socialist-Zionism

Snow falls in February

SNOW FALLS IN FEBRUARY AND COVERS THE
streets. And in Ussishkin Square, a man stands in
front of Bernhard and says:

Draga fodor uram, hogy az isten ovja meg,
    nagyon
remelem hogy a rabbi ur mar beszelt rolam,
    draga
uram, az utobbi idoben hozzam jutott a babeli
    talmud
egy borkoteses diszkiadasa, igazi mecije valaki
    aki
elutazott amerikaba hagyta nalam a sulya
    miatt. Olcson
adom es meg egy nagy micvat is tetszik
    csinalni. A
rabbi ur is azt mondta. Csalados ember vagyok
    kerem,
ket lanyt kell ferjhez adnom, de mit tudok en
    adni
nekik kerem, meg stafirungjuk sincs. . .

(More wonderful than the wonders

21

(MORE WONDERFUL THAN THE WONDERS
people sit and talk about, is the fact that they sit and
talk.) Sometimes Bernhard allows himself to eat
schnitzel. "Why," he thinks to himself, "is there
anything at all?" He cuts imaginary oranges and
squeezes juice from the pieces into glasses. His head
is full of obscene visions (only Gustav calls him
"Bernhard." Everyone else says "Mr. Stein"). He
doesn't remember Paula every day. And when children sing "The Almond Trees in Blossom" he sees,
in his mind's eye, cherry trees.

Against his will, Bernhard is proud

AGAINST HIS WILL, BERNHARD IS PROUD
that he knows the meaning of the word "Cockpit."
Visual memories come back to him (because of the
luminous light of Palestine) only sluggishly. He
thinks: "Who fills that fragment of space that my
father Sigmund's body once occupied?" "Where are
the sounds of my dead mother's voice preserved?"
"Is there an invisible line along the route that Bernhard Stein traveled on his way from Berlin to Palestine?" And he also thinks: "Can one remember
memories?" Only one or two odd recollections revolve in his head like a weathervane (such as the
time he said to an Arab: "Mafhum?"*).

*Do you understand?
(Arabic)

And even though Bernhard's mouth

AND EVEN THOUGH BERNHARD'S MOUTH
is full of teeth (just like a wolf's mouth, though
most of Bernhard's teeth are no longer whole), he
imagines himself the author of a realistic story (the
kind whose hero masturbates into the sink) but
interwoven with tender emotion, like a thin cord:

D.S. Gregory gently took Isabella's hand and
led her to the lamplight. "What you see," he
said, "is a skin fungus."

Whenever Bernhard meets Herzog

WHENEVER BERNHARD MEETS HERZOG, Herzog says, "Nu, what do you have to *say?*" And Bernhard answers out of habit: "very well, thank you." And when Bernhard resolves to answer Herzog: "What do *you* have to say?" Herzog (it had been ordained from the beginning of time that Herzog should have the upper hand) only says: "Nu?" And beyond Palestine, Hitler (who also has pubic hair on his body) invades everywhere and conquers whatever he lays his hands on. If Bernhard were younger he would go and fight. However, it seems to Bernhard ("Isabella left the room, but the scent of her body remained suspended in the air") that all these things had already taken place, exactly as they were happening now.

In March, the grass outside Jerusalem

25

IN MARCH, THE GRASS OUTSIDE JERUSALEM
revives. In one of his trouser pockets Bernhard finds
a note Paula had written for him:

> 3–4 lemons
> one rotel* of tomatoes (not soft)
> a few cucumbers
> an electric bulb

*An Arabic measure
of weight

"D.S. Gregory," Bernhard thinks, "should go to a
green-grocer to buy what Isabella wrote down, and
afterwards he must look for an electric bulb shop
and buy an electric bulb. But the bulb must burn
out or shatter as a kind of suggestion that Isabella is
dead." And he goes on thinking (like a man in a
trance): "Stalagmites rise from below, while stalac-
tites fall from above" and it seems to him that if he
reverses the words, the world will be thrown out of
order.

In May, the Queen of Holland flees

In May, the Queen of Holland flees Hitler's presence. At first, Bernhard thinks, the Queen fastens her boat to a post on the quayside at Dover. Then she gathers the hem of her skirt (clams had adhered to it) and enters a pipe shop (the smell of tobacco mixes with the smell of Wilhelmina). In June, other European kings come to London. Zog, King of Albania, comes with his wife and a babe in arms, and from the North, Haakon, King of Norway (whose forehead is wrinkled), comes. In his mind's eye, Bernhard sees them sit down and enjoy a hearty meal, and the President of Poland, the fat Radkivitz, sits with them. They begin with lentil soup. The king of Albania (who once met D.S. Gregory in Moscow) crudely slurps. Fat Radkivitz, a napkin around his neck, does his best to flatter Wilhelmina. Haakon, however, lets his spoon fall and sits lost in thought (the Albanian woman bares her breast in the corner of the room). Wilhelmina (her face pink) says: "I think we should talk about Hitler." "And I," Haakon says, "am of the opinion that you should have invited the Czech, Benes, as well." "Benes," fat Radkivitz says, "is a blemish," and the Albanian asks: "What is a blemish?" "A blemish," fat Radkivitz says, "is a sun-spot, a freckle. A stain that appears on one's face, as in the sentence 'The girl's face was covered with freckles.'"

If Gustav

IF GUSTAV (WHO DOES NOT KNOW WHO his mother and father were) raised his hands, Hitler would collapse. Gustav's long arms match the pattern of the cross whose ends bend in a single direction (that's why Gustav is the bent crucifix). Lately strange things have been happening, as when someone came in the dead of night and called out: "Herr Benjamin! The pipes have burst and the water is rising" . . . and Gustav said: "I get dressed and I come. . . ."

And I, Bernhard thinks

AND I, BERNHARD THINKS, WHAT DO I need? Nothing but a face and an egg. And when I have a face and an egg, I will dance in Palestine that dance called the Charleston (a Negro with a trumpet will stand alongside the river). Then the Pioneers (who settled Degania) will bow down to the ground and say: "Hallelujah! For this we have been waiting almost two thousand years! For Bernhard Stein (a fifty-year-old widower), son of Sigmund and Clara, to come from Berlin to Palestine and immerse himself in holy water!"

In July, Bernhard and Gustav go

IN JULY, BERNHARD AND GUSTAV GO TO the cinema and see (Gustav's knotty hands grasp the arms of the seat like the roots of a tree that have risen from the earth) Clark Gable and Vivien Leigh. Italian bombs fall on Haifa (though their number is considerably less than the number of German bombs falling, at that very moment, on London). And in August, one Frank Jackson stands on a corner in Mexico City. And when Trotsky comes he asks: Leib? and Trotsky says: It was once Leib. Then he asks: Bronstein? And Trotsky asks· Why do you ask? And Jackson says: What do you care? And Trotsky says: Yes! And Jackson asks: What do you mean, yes? And Trotsky says: Once it was Bronstein. And Jackson asks: And now? And Trotsky asks: What now? And Jackson says: You know! And Trotsky says: Now, it is Leon Trotsky. And Frank Jackson pulls out a revolver and fires four bullets at Leib Bronstein (the number of syllables in his later name). Everyone is convinced that Frank Jackson did what he did on Josef Stalin's orders. But actually Frank Jackson was born to Belgian parents in Persia. And Bernhard sees, in his mind's eye, Frank Jackson's parents in Isfahan, talking to each other in Flemish, and saying: "We'll call the baby Frank."

In Berlin, when he was a young man

IN BERLIN, WHEN HE WAS A YOUNG MAN, and afterwards in Jerusalem (not long after marrying Paula) Bernhard read in a book by some Dane or other that the Patriarch Abraham was the greatest of all men since he did not hesitate to sacrifice his son Isaac (the miracle of one man sprung from another) to God. And when Paula did not conceive (no fetus was formed in her womb), Bernhard thought to himself that Abraham would have done better if he had given his son Isaac to him (i.e., to Bernhard) and not to God. But lately Bernhard has been thinking: "Only Paula would have called the child by name, as if it were totally impossible for him to have any other name. But what would *I* do with the child? And the child, what would *he* do, when the time came, with *his* child? In the faces of children you can see that one day they will turn into rug merchants or post office clerks. Visions are nothing but sounds (I see a horse and think 'horse') and the flesh is transparent."

Gustav asks if he should join

31

GUSTAV ASKS IF HE SHOULD JOIN THE
British army (Herzog, or someone, told him that the
British were crying out for plumbers). But Bernhard
says: Und wie. . . Und wie. . . * (three times).
He thinks: If all the food and drink that have entered my mouth during my life were gathered in one
pile, how big would it be? And in view of this pile,
and considering it, and because of it, who is D.S.
Gregory and who is Isabella? (A giant bag of food
that has dreams, the son of Sigmund Stein. Right?)
He can observe Gustav from above. Summer's dryness has passed. Gustav is now Gustav-September.
From his (Bernhard's) glasses one of the lenses has
fallen out. Italian airplanes soar out of the exposed
eye. He bombs Tel Aviv. He kills Joseph Zalevianski (David Zalevianski's son. Right?) and Sisskind
and Tourgeman, and many, many more (he can kill
anyone he wants to). He doesn't need Paula (let her
say "Muschl" to someone else). He is a dirty saint
who pities only babes.

*And how . . .
(German)

Bernhard sees all kinds of widows

BERNHARD SEES ALL KINDS OF WIDOWS
and saleswomen in haberdashery shops, and imagines to himself that their names are Zelniker or
Fischbein. He thinks: "If the name of that one is
Zelniker or Fischbein, I want nothing to do with
her" (but in his imagination he does with them what
he pleases). He loves Mahatma Gandhi who sits by
his spinning wheel every day and spins (the dirty
old man!). And didn't God Himself order the
Prophet Hosea "Go, get yourself a wife of whore-
dom"? The Rabbis, he thinks, see the fingers of the
hand, but they don't see the toes of the feet (and
didn't Johanan Ben Zakai take off his shoes and put
his naked foot before the Sages, and that's why the
Sages decreed that the Law be determined according to him?). And Gustav, whose body is filled with
pipes of blood and carries, day after day, from house
to house, pipes (four-inch) of water, what would the
Rabbis do to *him*? Would they decree that he has
never existed but is only a parable (that Palestine
hoodwinks its inhabitants with imaginary sights)?
But Bernhard loves Gustav just because he is out of
the question (impossible). And what does Gustav
say at midnight? He says: "Bernhard," he says:
"Bernhard, tomorrow," he says: "Bernhard, tomorrow I'll" (and goes on: "mend your tap").

Bernhard doesn't know

BERNHARD DOESN'T KNOW IF BENBENISHTI
is back from Beirut, but he imagines to himself that
Benbenishti has, in fact, come back and asks if
everything turned out all right. He (i.e., Bernhard)
weighs his answer to Benbenishti and decides to ask
him if he met Oskar Kokoschka in Beirut. Benbenishti will be very sorry he did not meet Kokoschka.
He (i.e., Benbenishti) will have great difficulty
in pronouncing Kokoschka's name (his name is
"Kokoschka") but Bernhard will promise him (Benbenishti) to write to him (Oskar Kokoschka) and ask
him to look at Benbenishti's legs.

In that year the Atlantic Ocean

IN THAT YEAR THE ATLANTIC OCEAN FILLS up with an infinity of sounds. Igor Stravinsky sails across. Arnold Schoenberg sails across. And Paul Hindemith, and Béla Bartók, and Darius Milhaud, and Kurt Weill also cross (they are fleeing from Europe to the United States). And in December, the First Secretary of the Government (of Palestine) announces that the Government will no longer allow ram's horns, whose sound resembles the sound of an air-raid siren, to be blown in the synagogues. And Bernhard pictures to himself the Messiah coming (from Lisbon) to the sound of air-raid sirens. He'll go out the gates of the port and look around and see the writing on the wall (Kolondi and Sons—Building Materials) and say, "I have heard the voice of God cooing like a dove" and He'll go on foot to Allenby Street and take a taxi to Kiryat Motzkin and there, next to the grocery store, He'll meet Sarah Zitronenbaum. He'll say: "I am the Messiah, the Son of David" and Sarah will say: "Vos nokh?"* And Bernhard sees (in his mind's eye) that the rams' horns, which are no longer blown, go back on to the heads of the rams on the mountains and the rams, horns on their heads, call to the ewes with a blast and a wail to come to the act of love, but the females do not come (they turn their eyes to the air-raid sirens). And sometimes Bernhard too hears the sound of his dead mother Clara's voice. He thinks:

*And what else?
(Yiddish)

"All the voices in the world are coiled together like threads on one bobbin (that's invisible) and the bobbin turns and turns and the voices are heard."

And if, Bernhard thinks

AND IF, BERNHARD THINKS, IT OCCURRED to someone to write a book about my life, he would include the x-ray photograph of my chest. But Bernhard doesn't know what hold D.S. Gregory has on the world (where is *his* chest to be found?). If D.S. Gregory, thinks Bernhard, is in my mind, in whose mind am I? One way or another, D.S. Gregory was born in Moscow to Pavel and Yekaterina Sholochov. At his birth his face resembled Yekaterina's father's father, Gregory the Terrible. So Pavel resolved, in a light-hearted moment, that the name of the baby would be Gregory. Only later (to discharge their obligation to tradition) did they add the "D.S."—to suggest the names of other ancestors. Pavel had an airy disposition (he was in good spirits even when asleep), but about Yekaterina there stretched a thread of melancholy (there was stretched about her a thread of melancholy). On the face of it D.S. Gregory was a sad child but inside, among the chambers of his heart, he throbbed with joy. In days to come D.S. Gregory would say to Isabella: "You can see my mother in me from my inside outward, and my father from my outside inward."

By the time D.S. Gregory was born,

BY THE TIME D.S. GREGORY WAS BORN,
Gregory the Terrible was no longer among the living. But "Omurtag Khan and the Turko-Bulgarian
Kingdom" stood as a kind of memorial between the
icon of The Virgin of the Don and the icon of The
Holy Mother of Vladimir. "My grandfather," Yekaterina once said to D.S. Gregory, "who you are
named after, was a great scholar. In the whole of
Russia there was none so well versed in the history
of the Turko-Bulgarian Kingdoms." But only from
his father Pavel did D.S. Gregory learn why his
grandfather's father was called Gregory the Terrible. "From the day he reached maturity," Pavel
said, "he didn't put a razor to his skin (before then
his skin grew no hair) and in the middle of his life,
when his beard reached his knees, he gathered it up
in a purple velvet sack, which he carried under his
chin as is the custom of the Turko-Bulgarian Khans.
Most of his days Gregory the Terrible sat in a chair,
the bag of hair on his chest, and drank wine mixed
with water and blood from large silver cups (as was
the custom of the Turks)."

In his childhood Bernhard flew

IN HIS CHILDHOOD BERNHARD FLEW THE skies of Lapland on the back of a wild goose. Many strange and unexpected things happened to him and to Sigmund and Clara. Sigmund and Clara died and Bernhard came to Palestine by himself and married Paula, and Paula also died, and during all those years he never said "Ahalan,"* not even once. Those pot-bellies who strut about Palestine saying "Ahalan" disgust him. He wants to ask: "And Bernhard, the son of Sigmund and Clara, isn't he a man?" Sometimes the undersized and the skinny also say (unnaturally) "Ahalan." And when Bernhard sees them he feels ashamed, as if they had exposed themselves to him. And also the child D.S. Gregory, Bernhard thinks, is Nils Holgersson. If it were only possible to tell how the flesh touches the feathers . . .

*A greeting in Arabic common also among the Jews in Palestine

On the twenty-eighth of March

ON THE TWENTY-EIGHTH OF MARCH, A
great sea battle takes place. Two thousand four hundred Italians drown (five hundred others are fished
out). Not a single English sailor is injured (but
Virginia Woolf dies the same day). Bernhard tells
himself to count from one to two thousand four
hundred but gives up after a hundred and seventy.
He wonders if anyone said (before drowning)
"Arrivederci." Above the surface of the ocean the
air was filled with cries, but within (the width of one
little finger lower) silence prevailed. These sights do
not gladden Bernhard's heart, nor do they sadden it.
He forces himself to think of something else: Can
physicists explain smells?

And how, Bernhard thinks

AND HOW, BERNHARD THINKS, CAN A MAN
translate sights into words? Paula's thin legs before
she died. Gustav's facial expression. Let's suppose,
he thinks, that the Son of God has indeed come
down to the world (against his will Bernhard sees a
German take off his hat and ask Jesus: "Wie geht es
Ihrem Vater?"*). Surely he found innumerable
things on the surface of the earth, each completely
different from any other. If I were the Son of
God (or one of His apostles), Bernhard thinks, I
wouldn't preach to the Corinthians but rather to
one Corinthian or another, and not to the Hebrews
but to one Hebrew or another, and to each and every
one of the two thousand four hundred Romans.

Bernhard dreams

*How is your Father?
(German)

BERNHARD DREAMS THAT HE IS DEAD AND Paula is sitting on a high chair and shaking hands with the mourners. "In the last few weeks," Paula says (on her face a look of satisfaction), "he remembered every detail of his twenty-fourth year. He was twenty-four again. He didn't remember anything about the years that followed." And to someone else she says: "The injury to his head seemed small. I was the only one who knew it had spread inward."

In April, Rommel captures

IN APRIL, ROMMEL CAPTURES BENGHAZI. The English hold on to Tobruk. The Germans take over Yugoslavia. The English liberate Ethiopia (Bernhard thinks: "Let the midwives dig graves"). And on the seventh of May, Haile Selassie returns to Addis Ababa. Crowds of Ethiopians line the street and cheer the Emperor. But when the official car stops at the palace, the Emperor cannot open the door and his assistants are forced to pull him out through a window. On the twentieth of May, Rudolf Hess parachutes onto the estate of the Duke of Hamilton in Scotland. "I have come," he says, "to save mankind." "That's all very well," the Duke says, "but I don't see why, just for that, you have to destroy a rose bush."

The bag of hair and the cups of blood

THE BAG OF HAIR AND THE CUPS OF BLOOD
fire the imagination of the boy D.S. Gregory. He
imagines he is Omurtag Khan. He resolves to speak
only Turkish (this angers Yekaterina). He gallops
through the halls on a noble steed (at times Pavel
deigns to die under his sword). Things that are at
navel-level for everybody else are at eye-level to
him. And even though D.S. Gregory is nothing but
a figment of Bernhard's imagination, Bernhard cannot impose on him what will happen. Bernhard pictures in his imagination how Masha, the servant,
says "Put your hand here," and how D.S. Gregory
puts his palm on her knee (and she urges him:
"Higher, higher . . . "), but he realizes these
things aren't happening to D.S. Gregory, but to
himself.

Before D.S. Gregory was born

BEFORE D.S. GREGORY WAS BORN HIS
father Pavel crossed the ocean to America and took
part in the great battle at Saratoga. Fighting with
him were the Frenchman Lafayette and two Poles,
Kosciusko and Pulaski (and also a German named
Steuben). Kosciusko was killed in this battle, and
Pavel's left leg was severed by a blow from the
sword of an English cavalryman (Steuben also
died). But from that journey there remained in
Pavel's memory two sights: an oil painting *Portrait
of Ann Boylston* by John Singleton Copley, and a
man standing in the doorway of a house (fields of
wheat stretch out behind him) and saying: "I do not
live here."

Pavel would release the leather straps

PAVEL WOULD RELEASE THE LEATHER straps that held the false leg to his body, slap the reddened flesh with his palm (the leg's stump, freed from constraint, would wriggle like a happy baby) and say: "Well, here you are!" When D.S. Gregory reached maturity he made connections between things: The wooden leg (the wooden leg went up in flames when Napoleon stood at the gates of Moscow—the wagon drivers cried out: "Pavel Sholochov, where's your leg?") is Pavel's property. But in what way does his leg of flesh belong to him? If the leg of flesh is Pavel's property, then so are his stomach, his intestines, his eyes, and his head. The whole of Pavel is Pavel's property. And where is Pavel (whose organs are his property?). Let us assume, D.S. Gregory thought, that Pavel's leg of flesh is (in a certain sense) Pavel himself. But if Pavel is his leg and stomach and intestines, where is Pavel?

A nerve is a fiber

A NERVE IS A FIBER THAT SPREADS OUT from the brain in one's skull, or from the spinal cord. It transmits stimuli from every part of the body (as when one says, for example, "A guten

Have a good Sab-bath. (Yiddish)

Shabbes").* When you are thinking about them, the nerves are transmitting all kinds of stimuli (backwards and forwards). Bernhard thinks nerves

†*Nerves (German)*

are "Nerven."† Nerven are a lot of little dwarfs singing "Hi-Ho, Hi-Ho."

D.S. Gregory has to memorize

D.S. GREGORY HAS TO MEMORIZE THE personal pronouns in French. He pronounces "Je" and "Tu" correctly. But "Vous" and "Nous" sound in his mouth like "Nuss" and "Vuss." Yekaterina believes that D.S. Gregory is obliged to store a lot of French words in his memory.

Yekaterina's gloom (she believes in saints) is divided into fragments. When Yekaterina sews, D.S. Gregory sees Yekaterina's-needle-gloom and Yekaterina's-thread-gloom and Yekaterina's-cloth-gloom. But her voice is soft and gentle. She sighs and says: "There are things . . . " In days to come, after she jumps from her bedroom window, D.S. Gregory will see, in his mind's eye, Yekaterina flying and flying.

Lusts also disturb Herzog's peace of mind

LUSTS ALSO DISTURB HERZOG'S PEACE OF
mind (he is a kind of widow). The road jumps ahead
of him. He says, "Vos makht a yid,"* but something
is not right. Lizards run away from him. He flies
(but in a different fashion from Yekaterina) hither
and thither. His voice is thin. Hair grows away from
his body. Is there somewhere in the world (almost
certainly the world just exists, for no reason) someone who would say: "That sweat and that beard and
all the rest . . . it must be my Herzog."

Gustav says

*How are you?
(What is the Jew
doing?) (Yiddish)

GUSTAV SAYS: "IN TEL AVIV A MAN called David Rozenzweig killed another called Waxman." And in his mind's eye, Bernhard sees Waxman walking around and saying: Rozenzweig. Rozenzweig. Rozenzweig comes out of a drapery store and says: What? And Waxman says: Not you. And Rozenzweig asks: Who are you looking for? And Waxman says: David Rozenzweig. And Rozenzweig says: He's not here.

One hundred and forty-five German divisions

ONE HUNDRED AND FORTY-FIVE GERMAN divisions invade Russia, but Bernhard has a very fine power of discrimination. In the street he thinks (many times) "Ich möchte einen Raben haben."* And when he urinates he thinks: "And what is this body? It has been with me since Berlin. It passes water again and again. And it has already been here and there (they call it Bernhard Stein)." Sometimes he thinks: " 'Wait,' Bernhard Stein said, 'until the enemy appears on the skyline. Then aim slightly in front of the first figure.' The soldiers nodded their heads. Bernhard Stein turned and strode slowly back to the command tent, shoulders bent, as if carrying a heavy stone on his back."

*I want to have a raven /crow. (German)

Bernhard remembers some lines

BERNHARD REMEMBERS SOME LINES OF
poetry (he knows the words come from a poem by
Hugo von Hofmannsthal):

> Can it be
> That those days
> Are no more?
> Erased forever?
> As though they never were?

Gustav remembers: "I threw a rose into the sea."
It seems to him (to Gustav) that the words come
from an old German poem, but he is not certain. He
thinks: "Can it be that those days. . . How beautiful is Bernhard's poem." And Bernhard thinks: "I
threw a rose. . . How beautiful is Gustav's verse."

The dreams that D.S. Gregory sees

THE DREAMS THAT D.S. GREGORY SEES: Omurtag Khan sitting in a bath made of goat skin, and Pope Nicholas the First washing his body. Omurtag Khan says to himself: You must pay particular attention to the soles of your feet. Another dream: Yekaterina dancing in a large ballroom, alone. In a corner of the hall Pavel stands and shouts: Enough! Enough! His voice re-echoes between the walls, but Yekaterina continues to dance. Another dream: D.S. Gregory lies dead. Yekaterina and Pavel stand next to his body, but talk about other matters. Another dream: D.S. Gregory is flying. The earth pulls at his body and his wings are heavy, but he does not fall. People mustn't know he can fly. If they did, he could fly no more.

Did Yekaterina have lovers?

DID YEKATERINA HAVE LOVERS? ALL
that is known for sure is this: A young officer's pipe
stem touched the flesh of her arm. Did Yekaterina
soar? (Seven spheres encircle the world of bodies.)
Did Yekaterina plunge? (In the depths of the gaping
earth, like a funnel, is the Inferno. . . .) What is
beyond doubt is only this: That the soles of her feet
were scorched by a desert of burning sand, that her
body turned into a tree in a forest of human bodies,
that the hair on her head was sucked into a well of
tar, and that her stomach froze in a lake. Perhaps the
torments of Hell rang in her ears like the moaning of
desire. At night Yekaterina (fluids rising up between
her thighs) cried out: Da, Da, Da, Da, Da, Da, Da.

But when the moon is a thin line

BUT WHEN THE MOON IS A THIN LINE, Yekaterina sees a thin line. And whoever thinks that Yekaterina does not see a thin line, may his name be blotted out. And, Pavel sees a thin line and D.S. Gregory sees a thin line and Sigmund and Clara, when the moon is a thin line, see a thin line. And whoever thinks they do not see a thin line, may his name be blotted out. Cursed be anyone who thinks that Gustav and Herzog do not see a thin line when the moon is a thin line. When the moon is a thin line, Gustav sees a thin line and Herzog sees a thin line. And when the moon is a thin line, Bernhard also sees a thin line, and whoever thinks that Bernhard does not see a thin line, may his name be blotted out.

The things that enter one's skull

THE THINGS THAT ENTER ONE'S SKULL. All those years Yekaterina retained the memory of D.S. Gregory's small hand. Only this recollection saved her from insanity. Whither, she thought to herself, am I galloping, between these hairy legs? (and she jumped from the window). Now Yekaterina is an imaginary skeleton with an imaginary child in its eye sockets. And Paula, Bernhard thinks, is a real skeleton with an imaginary child in its eye sockets and so is my mother Clara, he thinks, and that child was me.

The word "kap" in Turko-Bulgarian

THE WORD "KAP" IN TURKO-BULGARIAN
means an image of a goddess (its sound in Turkish is
"kap," "kiab" in the Yakuti language, "kab" in
Mongolian, and "kep" in Hungarian). D.S. Gregory is strongly built. There is something Turko-
Bulgarian about his looks. The women of Moscow
already ask: "Whose son is this handsome lad?"
Even the prostitutes fancy him. Lately it has
seemed to D.S. Gregory—when he is awake, too—
that he can fly. He goes up (cheerful Pavel) and
down (gloomy Yekaterina), up and down, up and
down. "So this," he says to himself (in Russian), "is
the zest of life." Afterwards, when his body is
empty, dark thoughts grip him. "What does it all
mean? Futility. Man is alienated from man." Sometimes trivial incidents occur, as when a man of reli-
gion grabs the hem of his shirt and shouts, "A fire
shall descend from the skies and burn your flesh,"
and sometimes events heavy with fate occur, as
when a horse turns its neck and looks at him for a
long time without blinking an eyelid.

That beautiful man, Rabindranath Tagore

56

THAT BEAUTIFUL MAN, RABINDRANATH Tagore, is dead. Something, Bernhard thinks, brought about his death (flowers, moonlight). The smell of Bernhard's body hangs in the room on Prophets Street. His feet are heavy. When he goes to the toilet, he supports himself on the walls of the corridor. He urinates and counts up to three hundred (or he says "Silvia gib mit wasser" sixty times). He takes a bath once a week. He puts in his tea (because of the hard times) only one teaspoon of sugar. At times his heart skips a beat. But he knows, Oh-ho, he knows that a man who is alive cannot die (that "to be dead" is a contradiction in terms). He thinks: "As long as I live, I will not die (I will not die all my life)." When they burned Rabindranath Tagore's body, the fire at first grabbed hold of his white beard. His burning face resembled a bush with the colors of Autumn. But Gustav's poetry, Bernhard thinks, is not at all similar to the poetry of Rabindranath Tagore. Gustav's poetry is epic. More narrative in character, balanced (with great themes):

First you must lift a large barrel
And then you place a plastic pipe
In a larger pipe leading lengthwise
Through wooden walls to hot-water taps. . .

Gustav's face is like the face of a Swedish poet whose father was a clergyman. Gustav does not desire to reconquer Finland, but in order to burn his face one has to first pour kerosene over his chin.

Bernhard thinks: "What is missing

BERNHARD THINKS: "WHAT IS MISSING IN my life is Datum (though one should say Data, in the plural). I ought to greet all kinds of people, then something would happen." In the meantime he strikes tree trunks and stone posts with his hand (he passes his fingers over notice boards) in order to imprint real facts upon the world. "Even a cough," he thinks, "somehow remains on record." But Bernhard will (in the end) have the privilege of being buried in Palestine, for two reasons: A. He saw things (a bottle of oil, a pine cone). B. He wandered about at the head of large armies and sang (soundlessly) Schubert's song:

> Where are you, where are you,
> My beloved country?
> That I sought, and imagined,
> Yet never knew.

He sees a woman

HE SEES A WOMAN WHO SPREADS HER fingers in the air, her hands cupped upwards. Her neck (she is an atheist) is damp with sweat. She cries for no reason (her joy finds no body to give it shape). Yekaterina cries for no reason but her neck is not damp with sweat. Paula's neck is damp with sweat but she does not spread her fingers in the air, and Clara spreads her fingers in the air but her hands are not cupped. The woman that Bernhard sees (in his mind's eye) is looking for fallen stars.

All the forces of flesh and spirit

ALL THE FORCES OF FLESH AND SPIRIT
are entangled in Yekaterina, but Pavel cannot be
cruel to her and say, "You and I are nothing but fig-
ures in the imagination of a fickle author." When
the English cavalryman severed his leg (at Saratoga)
Pavel screamed in pain. But at that very moment he
understood that anywhere in the world you can cut
it up and it will still remain whole. When he touches
something solid and hard (a cabinet or a vase) he
says to himself: "Even though this dream is a little
more tangible than nighttime dreams, it has no reality." He is filled with an empty joy. He thinks: "This
is good and this is also good." And since the Gospel
is good tidings he asks the servant girl to go up and
down between his legs (he consoles Yekaterina in
roundabout ways, like asking her: "Where did you
leave my garters?").

In days to come D.S. Gregory will think

IN DAYS TO COME D.S. GREGORY WILL think (as if he were inside a novel that he himself was writing): "When I saw Isabella I heard the sound of butterfly wings. She was leaning on the hedge of the Girls' Academy, alone. I thought to myself: 'The Holy Trinity.' Eyes grey as smoke. . ." But since he has not yet met Isabella (in the meantime, when he copulates, he hears only the sound of the wings of large swamp birds), he is amazed that the stars move in their courses, or he thinks: "In Budapest at this very moment, thousands of Hungarians are clipping their toenails."

The sun and the moon are connected

61

THE SUN AND THE MOON ARE CONNECTED
to the two ends of a single cord. When one rises the
other sets and vice versa. Prayers don't help but a
world without Herzog is inconceivable. Bernhard
thinks: "Damn the German (my poor father, Sigmund) who says 'Ja' and 'Nein' as though flesh were
not grass. As if there had been (perhaps) some disorder at first, but afterwards Space transformed itself (and Time flowed) at equal intervals only in
order that Herr Mannheim or Frau Appenzeller
might come into the world to do what they do."
Herzog scorns sights that are not useful. Shrieking
birds clash inside his body. But he doesn't say "Ja"
and "Nein" (he says "Yo" and "Neyn").

When the Japanese bomb Pearl Harbor

WHEN THE JAPANESE BOMB PEARL HARBOR, the ships anchored in Bernhard's head go up in flames. Time is back to front. The train that travelled (in nineteen hundred and twenty-five) from Berlin to Hamburg travels (the engine in the rear) from Hamburg to Berlin. You can see again (in an inverted vision, from outside inwards) the woman that Bernhard loved. They go (facing the street) inside a hotel. Their lips separate again and again. Their words are reversed as in mirror writing. But the beautiful body of the woman from Hamburg (her flesh is not flesh) is the same. Blessed art Thou our Lord, King of the Universe who takes (in nineteen hundred and twenty-five) Bernhard, the son of Sigmund and Clara Stein, to Hamburg and there arranges for him to meet, by the Grace of God, Anne Marie and had she not been Catholic, Bernhard could have held her hand in his and flown (four wing-power) over the tramcars and pedestrians, seeing through the (third and fourth floor) windows the women of Hamburg spreading red-and-white checkered tablecloths and pouring oxtail soup into large bowls.

The laces of Bernhard's shoes

THE LACES OF BERNHARD'S SHOES ARE
Bernhard's shoelaces and nobody else's. What's
more, the heavy black shoes are the shoes that Bernhard and nobody else puts on his bare feet (to be
precise, Bernhard first puts on stockings and only
afterwards, over his stockings, his shoes). But the
shoelaces are not the shoes themselves, nor are they
the stockings, and certainly not Bernhard's bare
feet, which are under the stockings. The shoelaces
don't *have* to be in Bernhard's shoes. They could, if
they wanted to, leave Bernhard's shoes and go
somewhere else entirely, and Bernhard would be left
with just his shoes, without laces. Let's imagine that
the shoe laces (or one lace, at least) go to Berlin and
there, in Berlin, in Bismarckplatz for example,
someone says: "Look, Look! Isn't that the shoelace
of Bernhard, Sigmund Stein's little boy?"

The heart constantly moves

THE HEART CONSTANTLY MOVES WITHIN the blood and within the flesh. It isn't possible to talk about Herzog by starting from the beginning (i.e., in sequence, or one thing after another). No one knows the purpose of things (apart from the Jewish Agency and Roosevelt). Sigmund is dead and Clara is dead and Bernhard will die. Things are simpler than people think. Every man has his face and his egg. Even the fastidious reader takes off his trousers, puts them on, and takes them off again. Anger and dissent do great harm to one's earnings. Bugs called vantsn* must be driven away or killed. Places where they hide must be smeared with a mixture of the bile of a bull and vinegar, or a very strong vinegar, the kind called Esik-Esentsie (or essence of vinegar). God is without beginning and without end (i.e., his age is infinite. Not that he is without purpose). On Friday morning (while Herzog is still asleep) his wife will take a handful of crushed salt and a little quicklime ground up small, and prepare nineteen black peppers, and put all this in a clay pot, and place the pot inside a hot oven and say as follows: Azoy vi dos ales vos do in der shterts ligt brent. Azoy zol brenen dos harts fun mayn man. Un er zol mikh lib hobn mit a shtark libshaft oyf eivig, Amen Selah.†

*Bed bugs (Yiddish)

†As all of this burns in the fire let my husband's heart burn. And he will love me with a great love, forever. (Yiddish)

The Germans form an alliance

The Germans form an alliance with
Italy and Japan. The Japanese invade Burma and
the Solomon Islands. The Nazi leaders gather at
Wannsee and decide to exterminate the Jews (fewer
and fewer Jews remain in the world) and in Ankara
two Russian communists make an attempt on the
life of the German diplomat von Papen. One Russian communist stands at the end of the alley, and
the other Russian communist places himself in
front of von Papen. "Von Pafen," the Russian
communist says, "your fate is sealed." "Von
Papen," the German corrects him. "That's not important," the Russian communist says. "Quickly!"
whispers the Russian communist standing at the
end of the alley. "It certainly is," von Papen says.
"Is what?" the Russian communist asks. "Important," von Papen says.

(And in Palestine) Bernhard's flesh

(AND IN PALESTINE) BERNHARD'S FLESH
is torn into pieces. He contemplates divine myster-
ies. At times his ears hear apocalyptic melodies:

> The almond tree's in flower
> Hitler needs a shower
> Little birds fly higher
> Singing "Look, Messiah!"

He thinks: "For an infinite number of years earth
and water and fire and air merged and separated and
merged again until the complete form of Gustav
materialized. Now that he has materialized, someone has to take care that he doesn't die." When they
Analysis (German) talk about Analyse* (the dissecting of something
complex and complicated like, for example, sleep or
fainting or death) Gustav thinks they are talking
about Anne Liese. Anne Liese has two milk nipples. Her legs are thin and delicate (but strong). She
resembles an antelope. Her eyes are large. Their
color is grey like the color of smoke (exactly like
Isabella's eyes). If Gustav had had a sister like Anne
Liese she would have read him ancient war stories
during the long winter nights. "And in the end," she
would have said, "Odysseus returns to Penelope"
and doves would have risen from Gustav's head.

Care must also be taken

CARE MUST ALSO BE TAKEN TO SEE THAT
Herzog does not die. At least let him utter a spell
against danger (and if *he* cannot, let someone else
utter it in his place): "I beseech you in the name of
God, the Lord of Hosts, and in the name of Tesa
Mesa Nesa that I be saved (or if someone else says
it, that 'Herzog be saved') from every type of misfortune and danger. Amen Selah, for ever and ever."
Or let another spell be uttered: "May the heads of
my enemies become the heads of donkeys, and my
head (or 'Herzog's head') the head of a lion. May
their tongues become the tongues of swine, and my
tongue ('Herzog's tongue') the tongue of a king.
May the Angel Yohach preserve me ('Herzog'), may
the Almighty save me ('Herzog'), let there be
Taftafya between us." Or as a talisman let him carry
a snake's head in his belt, and tie the eye of a chicken
to his right side. Or let him go to a kibbutz and
everyone will see (where they bathe communally)
his male organ, and by the power of this sight nothing shall happen to him that doesn't happen to
everyone else.

In the book by Wilhelm Busch

IN THE BOOK BY WILHELM BUSCH, BERNHARD
reads the fable of the raven Hans Huckebein. Hans
Huckebein upsets the basket of eggs and bites Aunt
Lotte's nose. But when he drinks to excess and a
string of wool gets wrapped around his neck,
Bernhard feels sad. Alas for those who are lost and
gone forever. He (i.e., Bernhard) tries to picture in
his mind the love between D.S. Gregory and Isabella, but doesn't know how to do it (sights and
smells deceive him). The more he thinks of peg-
legged Pavel, the fonder he grows of him. He (i.e.,
Pavel) slaps the buttocks of servant girls whose flesh
(that soft material that covers the skeleton) is filled
with muscle fibers and nerves and sinews and blood
vessels and fat, and he thinks to himself: "If life is
but a dream, it had better be a good one." His desires do not decrease in the afternoon hours. He says
to D.S. Gregory: "You must always go directly to
the heart of things. The world, my son, is nothing
but legs."

In his mind's eye Bernhard sees

IN HIS MIND'S EYE BERNHARD SEES STRANGE
visions, like being sealed inside a pot (but the pot is
the whole world) or scholars from the four corners
of the earth gathering and debating how to explain
"chimney," and when they are unable to do so he
(i.e., Bernhard) gets to his feet and says: "A hole in
the roof through which smoke escapes" and all of
them are struck dumb. Kefir delights his palate. He
thinks: "Do things happen by chance?" When he
feels the urge for kefir (sour milk in a long-necked
bottle), he goes to the grocery store. In his room on
Prophets Street he takes a long-handled spoon
(whoever doesn't have such a spoon cannot eat kefir,
or can eat only half of it) and inserts it into the neck
of the bottle. "Perhaps," he thinks, "things do happen by chance, but they don't happen any *other*
way. Where Bernhard eats kefir, the only thing that
can happen is what actually does happen (i.e., Bernhard eats kefir)."

He imagines to himself

HE IMAGINES TO HIMSELF THAT HE IS ONCE again in the house on Strauss Street. The baby that was not born to Paula is born from his own stomach, and he gives the baby to Paula and Paula places it, naked as it was born, on her stomach, flesh to flesh. The baby has a tiny soul and his lemon tree smell fills the house (but the baby cries and Bernhard doesn't know what to do). His imaginings take shape as though they were really in this world. But the visions that are only in his mind are feebler. He pines for Paula's old age (i.e., for the life that would have been if she hadn't died). She seems to be by his side. Trivial things occur (as when she says "Nicht so"* when he is having difficulty opening an umbrella). He thinks all kinds of thoughts (his thoughts and those thoughts he thinks about his thoughts). And since he has lost one thing, he loathes every thing (nothing else is Paula). He thinks: "If I were an imaginary person, the pain I feel wouldn't be so strong."

*Not that way (German)

When Moscow went up in flames

71

WHEN MOSCOW WENT UP IN FLAMES, A great bird was pictured in the clouds. Pavel's severed leg hung in the air (October snows were falling). In the North, where the wagons were headed, there was silence. "Yekaterina," Pavel suddenly said, "It isn't always . . ." Afterwards he said: "But. . . ," and finally he said: "Now . . ." "Vite! Vite!"* French soldiers called out (to each other) in the burnt-out city.

*Quickly, quickly (French)

Pavel's body

PAVEL'S BODY FELL FORWARD. HIS FACE rested in the space that his missing leg had left vacant. Did darkness fall on his inner visions? Did the wheat field that he saw turn black? Was the true meaning of life finally revealed to him (a distant figure that everything emanates from)? The horses, at any rate, charged on. And when Yekaterina saw that Pavel was emptied (D.S. Gregory was wandering with a different convoy), she stuck her head out of the carriage window and shouted "Stop!" "Impossible, my Lady," the drivers shouted. "It's impossible to stop the whole caravan." "Stop!" Yekaterina shouted a second time (she wished to get away from the corpse) "Sholochov is dead." But when they removed Pavel's body to a different carriage and she remained alone, Yekaterina thought to herself that these things were not really happening. His death, she thought, is nothing but one of his pranks (in days to come saints would appear in her dreams and urge her to prostitute herself).

When they buried Pavel

WHEN THEY BURIED PAVEL,
He was already blue.
A person loved.
Either he sliced them
Or they sliced him.
From others he asked only what
He would anyway have received.
And though to Yekaterina's nostrils
His smell was not like his smell
To D.S. Gregory's,
Pavel did have
A smell of his own.
Now he will wear
A more airy body (mostly thoughts)
And chase celestial maids.
He died easily
(A generation before his death
Vultures had eaten the flesh of his leg)
And he shall live many years
After his death.

What happens in April

WHAT HAPPENS IN APRIL? THE AMERICANS
bomb Tokyo. Benbenishti's honor is impugned.
Professor Hermann Strauss of Berlin takes his own
life. Herzog eats cheese and onions. His toes are
stuffed into shoes. He says, "Veys ikh vos"* (but
whoever thinks that he stinks, stinks himself). In
April Bernhard's life is diluted, at last, into a kind of
time solvent. He becomes acquainted with Mrs.
Neuwirth. People say "How are you, Mr. Stein?"
(Like this, for example: Bernhard is strolling down
Abarbanel Street and someone is coming up. And as
this person passes, he says, "How are you, Mr.
Stein?") Mighty breasts rest on the iron railing of a
balcony on Zunz Street. Bernhard also sees, here
and there, cats that cannot logically be said to exist
(thought does not give birth to them). His heart is
filled with happiness: Oh, the trees. Oh, the houses.
He thinks: "'Stolpern'—'to stumble'—is 'lim-od'
in Hebrew. 'Lim' is like in 'limon,' Hebrew for
'lemon.' 'Od,' Hebrew for 'more,' is 'Noch' in German. 'Od-limon' another lemon. Or backwards—
'limon-od,' but without. . . 'on.'" (Or he thinks:
"Did my mother Clara also have a baby that died?
Memories vanish and all that remain are sensations
of memory.") He sees (together with Gustav) the
film "Bambi." Gustav's hand is suspended in the air
of the Atara café, and where his hand ends there's a
cheesecake. Bernhard thinks: "Here is Gustav's
hand in April." Things that were obscure suddenly
become clear, in total simplicity.

"Sometimes, Mr. Stein,"

*What do I know?
(Yiddish)

"Sometimes, Mr. Stein," Mrs. Neuwirth says, "a man has to give up his dreams and be satisfied with what life has to offer." Mrs. Neuwirth was widowed while still in Vienna but in his mind's eye Bernhard sees Kurt Neuwirth sitting behind his desk while Elvira shakes his books, one by one, and blows away dust from their pages. "And I told her," she says, "that she is absolutely right, and he's mistaken." Kurt lifts his eyes from his papers (his pipe is in the pipe stand on the edge of the desk) and says: "Elvira!" From his tone Elvira knows she should put her duster down. She folds her hands near her groin, more or less. Kurt says: "Never. Never (he says) is a person completely right and his opponent absolutely wrong." "No?" Elvira wonders. "No!" Kurt says, "since truth is never absolute. It is never more than partial." And Elvira knows that in days to come, when Kurt is dead (how's that for absolute truth) she too will make use of this expression. "Alright," Bernhard says, "but there's no reason why a man shouldn't dream." "There certainly is," Mrs. Neuwirth says. "If dreams stand between him and reality."

Mrs. Neuwirth says

Mrs. Neuwirth says: "Listen Mr. Stein" (at first the flash of silver from the scales came and went, came again and went, even though the basin was only one or two feet deep—when the rolling pin crushed its skull, the carp ceased to think, but its body quivered in Elvira's shopping bag):

*On a high pasture in the North / Stands a lonely pine / Covered with a blanket of frost and snow / It sleeps and dreams and trembles (Hebrew - a poem by Heine)

†It can't be (German)

Bema'are giv'ah batsafon
Omed oren boded
Oteh sut kfor vasheleg
Rodem cholem ro'ed*

"What's that?" Bernhard asks. "Heinrich Heine," Mrs. Neuwirth says, "in Palestine." "Unmöglich,"† Bernhard says, "what is 'sut'?" "That," Mrs. Neuwirth says, "is Hebrew for 'Decke,' a blanket." "But," Bernhard says, "Heine's tree doesn't tremble." "Right," Elvira says, "Heine's tree doesn't tremble. It just sleeps and dreams."

Without Pavel

WITHOUT PAVEL ALL THE SIGHTS THAT Yekaterina sees are Pavel-less (without Pavel it's a Pavel-less world). But at the end of the months of mourning, Pavel dons a body of memory. At times Yekaterina sees him, in her mind's eye, with his leg missing, and at times she sees him standing on both legs (there is no difference in weight between the two images). Yekaterina teaches herself to smirk. Previously (before Pavel's death) she knew that there were human beings in the Gospel apart from the Holy Virgin. But then she didn't picture circus dwarfs, hairy Jews, and iron-clad warriors. In December, in the middle of the night, Yekaterina turns into a mare, and a tiger-headed prince rides on her back. At dawn her body aches (they pinched her nipples, kneaded her thighs, pulled her hair, and sank their nails into her flesh) from the dream. She covers her body with a red robe and stares (her pubic hair is wet) at the snow flakes through the window glass.

Elvira Neuwirth talks of

ELVIRA NEUWIRTH TALKS OF SPIRITUAL
matters (she exudes a kind of supplication) but
Bernhard longs for real conversation. ("Forty years
ago," John said, "the eastern end of the Valley was a
total wasteland." "Indeed," Henry said, "many
years have passed. . . ," "since," John cut him off,
"two runny-nosed youngsters, one named Henry
and the other named John, were competing for the
favors of a certain young lady. . . ," "Blast it!"
Henry cried, his face flushed with excitement,
"What was her name? . . .") And when he orders
kefir for himself he adds, "Well, how are things Mr.
Shereshevsky?" "Men lebt,"* Shereshevsky says.
"Men lebt. That's all?"

*One lives / all right
(Yiddish)

The swamp bird screeches

THE SWAMP BIRD SCREECHES (SHAK-SHAK)
in wet fields, near reservoirs. Since only Gustav, the
crucified, and the swamp bird exist in the world, the
Gospel is heard (there are no other tidings—only
the sound of the swamp bird). People do not understand. Gustav was born and now he is taking a bath.
And when he gets out of the water (in nineteen hundred and forty-two a flame was burning at the bottom of the boiler) he dries his one and only body. It's
impossible to describe such things in words. Wherever Gustav goes (his head cuts through space) he
carries his male organ. It is not his fault that he is in
Palestine. People should say only what is necessary
(for instance, that a clarinet is larger than an oboe)
or worry about Elvira Neuwirth.

The King of the Danes

THE KING OF THE DANES, CHRISTIAN THE Tenth, visits a synagogue in Copenhagen and declares: "If the Jews are ordered to wear the yellow badge, then we shall all wear it." Yellow Christian the Great says "Juder"* with a kind of trilling of the vowel that is not directed against the Jews (it is in the nature of the Danish language). And what does Christian the Tenth think? "If the Jews," Christian thinks, "have to wear the yellow badge, we shall all," he thinks, "including me, wear it." The chief rabbi of the Jews of Denmark says a prayer for the health of the king. "And now," Christian thinks (Jews wearing prayer shawls gather round him), "they are praying for my health in that ancient language." Women, their heads covered with lace, peer through the glass.

*Jews (Danish)

The Germans advance

THE GERMANS ADVANCE ON ALEXANDRIA.
The English retreat to El Alamein. At night Elvira
Neuwirth covers her stomach with a white sheet.
"Der Bauch von Elvira Neuwirth."* This is a great
and powerful thought. In his mind's eye Bernhard
sees the prophet Jonah and Geppetto (they have
only one candle) leaning, pale-faced, on the white
ribs. He lusts for her inner organs, in that place
where she is dark and moist (and is not Elvira).

*The stomach of
Elvira Neuwirth
(German)

Alas, Elvira grows old

ALAS, ELVIRA GROWS OLD BUT HER IMAGE in the photograph does not change at all. If she had accepted Max Berthof's proposal, he (and not Kurt Neuwirth) would have married her. One way or another, her stomach would still have contracted and stretched all those years. In his mind's eye Bernhard sees his father Sigmund sitting in front of the wardrobe with his feet inside the shoe drawer. When he said to the German carpenter, "The wardrobe must also have a drawer for feet," Clara corrected him at once and said "shoes," but engraved in Bernhard's memory were Sigmund's exact words (Bernhard thought: "My father will draw his strength from inside the drawer"). Once a day, at about nine o'clock in the morning, Elvira brews camomile tea (she stands in the kitchen and brews camomile tea).

In the beginning of November

IN THE BEGINNING OF NOVEMBER THE English win the battle of El Alamein. Elvira Neuwirth spreads a woolen blanket over the white sheet. In Jerusalem (morning and evening) the cold already penetrates to the bones. At night Elvira Neuwirth's bones lie under the white sheet. Someone should worry about Elvira catching a chill (let the children sing "Elvira" instead of "David, King of Israel"). In the meantime her bones are alive (there is bone marrow in them). The body of another person should lie on Elvira's body.

In Palestine the sun turns

IN PALESTINE THE SUN TURNS UPSIDE DOWN
in the sky. Every second person is Gross (half-
ironed) standing next to a shop and explaining
everything himself. Gross gives birth to a smaller
Gross who in turn gives birth to his own Gross.
When you say to Gross "I dare you," he knows exactly what you mean. You could subdue Gross in
the royal court in Oslo (but it's difficult to tempt
Gross to go there). Even those who say "What's
new?" in Hebrew (or sing "Let Us Draw Water
from the Wells of Israel"), half of them are Gross.
Elvira must take care. A Viennese woman who
married a Gross is today only the shadow of herself.
She gave birth to children who look like Gross and
she got used to saying things that are not true
(Gross has a Croatian life-force) in a style that is
un-Viennese.

Bernhard's visionary gifts

85

BERNHARD'S VISIONARY GIFTS FALL SHORT
of those possessed by Russians (he is not Berl
Katzenelson).* Sometimes he loves Palestine and
sometimes not. If only it were a little darker and its
inhabitants (like in the villages of Bavaria) somewhat feeble-minded. . . . He sees himself as a
prophet standing on a high mountain and saying
"This is the Word of God etcetera, etcetera" (multi-
tudes gather at the foot of the mountain), but actually he thinks about meaningless things (that, for
example, "Schnurrbart"† is in Hebrew "a beard-
thread") and weighty matters (such as "What am
I?") as if they were all the same.

*A Zionist leader
(1887–1944)

†Moustache
(German)

He wants to picture in his imagination

HE WANTS TO PICTURE IN HIS IMAGINATION
the love between D.S. Gregory and Isabella, but all
he sees are sailing ships and hippopotamuses. Hitler
turned the world upside down. His (Bernhard's)
thoughts are disordered. He thinks: "You must
punish a man who cuts off the leg of a pig. A pig
goes about on four legs. If one leg is missing, it has a
hard time keeping its balance. You shouldn't cut off
the leg of a man who cuts off the leg of a pig (or at
least, not the whole leg), but you should cause him
pain or sorrow. People cut off a pig's leg (or a cow's)
and at the same time talk about the Jewish Agency
or the shop prices. Butchers and clerks masturbate.
There is no mammal but man (and no bird or fish
either) that does such different things at one and the
same time or even one after another. No pig has obscene imaginings which cause it to spill its seed."

In January Bernhard sees

IN JANUARY BERNHARD SEES "SNOW WHITE
and the Seven Dwarfs" (with Gustav). Snow
White's face is like Anne Marie's (in Hamburg in
nineteen hundred and twenty-five). When the
prince kisses Snow White, she opens her eyes and
steps out of the glass coffin. Benbenishti is also sitting in the Atara café. Gustav says "Gustav Benjamin" and Benbenishti says "Benbenishti." Bernhard wants to ask Benbenishti if Oskar Kokoschka
has already looked at his legs, but there is a man sitting at Benbenishti's table with the face of a croco-
dile. Bernhard imagines to himself that Benbenishti
is saying:

> Oh my, Herr Zwirn,
> When winter comes,
> Where shall I find,
> The flower,
> And the heat of the sun?

The Russians announce

THE RUSSIANS ANNOUNCE A GREAT VICTORY at Stalingrad. They killed three hundred and thirty thousand Germans and Romanians. Bernhard is happy, but doesn't understand what the Romanians were doing there (he supposes they went because of a woman named Mrs. Knoller). In the room on Prophets Street he is sometimes aware of the smell of breaking wind (not his). Frühling! Frühling.* How many years, Bernhard thinks, do I have left to live? (Surely Elvira made herself a list of all the parts of her body),

*Spring (German)

Mr. Moller and Mr. Zoller
Even though their willies froze
Lie on top of Mrs. Knoller
(One after the other).

Scholars seek

SCHOLARS SEEK AN IMAGINARY TRUTH (they cannot explain a spit). Alfonso is so fat he can split himself up and sell sunflower seeds in several places in Jerusalem. Fraulein Schmidt is to be found in only one place (in Berlin in nineteen hundred and nineteen—she sees to it that everyone says "pillow" properly, the way the English pronounce the word). More than anything, Fraulein Schmidt gets angry when a pupil picks his nose ("Peter Stahl," she says, "I may have succeeded in teaching you a little English, but there are things of greater importance. . ."). It is not the similarity to the sexual act (the insertion of a long organ inside a bodily cavity) that annoys Fraulein Schmidt, so much as the slackness, taking the easy way (". . . like, for example, a man having a moral backbone since, at times, Mr. Peter Stahl, one is obliged to do things the hard way"). "Mein Gott," Bernhard thinks to himself, "if Fraulein Schmidt saw Alfonso, she wouldn't believe her eyes."

Sometimes a sharp pain

SOMETIMES A SHARP PAIN KNIFES THROUGH
Bernhard's stomach. He inhales air and exhales air
(he breathes). Gustav appears, dewdrops on his
forehead, as if he has come from nowhere. What is
this sudden appearance of Gustav? What is the
meaning of the sharp pain? Ultimately, everything
is bound to come to an end, not in sorrow but rather
in infinite joy,

> Doctor Zoller and Doctor Moller,
> Although their willie's thin
> Will lay Mrs. Knoller
> Without and within.

In 1812, between the 13th and 18th of September

IN 1812, BETWEEN THE 13TH AND 18TH of September, three quarters of the buildings of Moscow burnt down (3/20th every day) and on the 20th of October, one day after the French retreated from Moscow (a sick Frenchman gave himself up), the Russians returned. A barrel of ink would not suffice to describe how the architect Osip Bove stood on a hill and looked out over the burnt city. The autumn wind stirred his whiskers. "I," Osip Bove said to himself (he clenched his jaw), "shall rebuild Moscow."

The image of the moon in water

THE IMAGE OF THE MOON IN WATER IS circular. But Osip Bove did not like the circular body of his wife. "The circle," he thought, "is an area on a plane enclosed by a curve that is everywhere equidistant from the center." And he also thought: "She is not only Circulus, but also Circulus Vitiosus (an error, a thing that has no way out)." He wanted the buildings he rebuilt to rise higher and higher. Nevertheless, he was something of a nuisance (his skin was pink, he talked about stockings as if they were landscapes). "Osip Bove," Yekaterina thought, "is a kind of positive of Pavel Sholochov. Osip sees the buildings, while dead Pavel saw the space within."

Did Yekaterina say to herself

DID YEKATERINA SAY TO HERSELF, A MOMENT before she moved, "Within the instant I shall move"? Suddenly, Yekaterina moved. How did Yekaterina move? After all, before she moved she wasn't moving. Was there already within her, in the unmoving Yekaterina, the forthcoming movement? And if she intended to move did she also want that intent? Ay, ay, Yekaterina spreads her legs. She must not be prosecuted. Before she spread her legs, she did not spread them, and after spreading her legs she did not spread them. No one understands these changes. Osip Bove introduced himself and said: "Osip Bove—Architect." But at night he stuck his whiskers between Yekaterina's legs until her pubic hair touched his nose (Yekaterina said: "No, Osip, no"). Afterwards Yekaterina had peaceful dreams. (Gravediggers digging a hole. Field mice quietly peeping.)

Gustav's fingernails

GUSTAV'S FINGERNAILS ACCOMPANY HIM
all the days of his life. When they are cut, they grow
again and cover the flesh on his fingers. On the
thumb of Gustav's right hand there is a fingernail
(its name is Gustav). On the thumb of Gustav's left
hand there is a fingernail (its name is Gustav). On
the forefinger of Gustav's right hand there is a fingernail (its name is Gustav). On the forefinger of
Gustav's left hand there is a fingernail (its name is
Gustav). On the middle finger of Gustav's right
there is a fingernail (its name is Gustav). On the
middle finger of Gustav's left hand there is a fingernail (its name is Gustav). On the ring finger of Gustav's right hand there is a fingernail (its name is
Gustav), and on the ring finger of Gustav's left hand
there is a fingernail (its name is Gustav). On the little finger of Gustav's right hand there is a fingernail
and its name is Gustav. If Gustav also had a fingernail on the little finger of his left hand, the name of
that fingernail would be Gustav. But Gustav does
not have a little finger on his left hand (the little finger of his left hand was severed in Rechavia).* Oh,
God! Preserve Gustav's nine fingers. Surely, Gustav
is not a wolf. If it weren't for his fingernails, he
couldn't tighten the pipe wrench properly (the flesh
of his fingers would be crushed).

*A quarter in
Jerusalem

People believe

PEOPLE BELIEVE THAT THE CORRECT ORDER
is as follows:

1. Truth (in light blue).
2. History (Napoleon, the Jews, etc.).
3. Living persons (Bernard Shaw and others).
4. Animals and Things.

But the correct order is different. It's impossible to say what it is (if it were known, it would be thrown into disorder). There are things that are precisely equivalent to Gustav's fingernails (for example, the Pope and the London Botanical Gardens). If Gustav had only one fingernail, you could visualize Gustav's life as the plot of a novel (from the beginning of the fingernail to the end). But it's difficult to think of a plot for nine fingernails. Besides, if you told Gustav that "Alilah"* is a Hebrew word he would be very surprised. He knows the word "Sipur"† (in his mouth it sounds like this: "Sipua"). The marching song of this story (about Bernhard and Gustav and all that) is "The Song of Gustav's Nine Fingernails."

*Plot (Hebrew)

†Story (Hebrew)

In March Mahatma Gandhi

IN MARCH MAHATMA GANDHI COMMITS himself to a fast. Sergei Rachmaninoff weakens and dies. And, at the same time as King Boris of Bulgaria (the eldest son of the great prince of Bulgaria, Ferdinand the First and his wife, Maria-Louisa, of the house of Bourbon-Parma) meets with Hitler (Schicklgruber), Eva Braun shows Giovanna Queen of Bulgaria (the daughter of Vittorio Emanuelle the Third, King of Italy) some crystal vases. "And this one," she says, "is especially fine." Outside, rain mixed with hail is falling.

Elvira Neuwirth loves Schiller

Elvira Neuwirth loves Schiller though actually (she says) she loves Heine even more. "It's simply unbelievable," Bernhard thinks, "that you also need legs to love Heine." Sometimes legs are no more than a proverb (as when one says "A lie hath no legs") but Elvira's legs are covered with fine hair (not very old). Bernhard imagines that Elvira is a prostitute who has taught herself how to say "Eigentlich"* in the right place. Any man who exposes her real nature will earn a wonderful reward (Elvira will be happy, at last, to be herself).

*Actually (German)

Time is reversed

TIME IS REVERSED WHEN BERNHARD IS IN Tel Aviv. The sight of the sea is the beginning of the journey. Afterwards Bernhard travels backwards. In Mograbi Square he takes a sausage out of his stomach and gives it back to Hans. Hans tells him his life story from the time he sold sausages in Palestine until he became (a younger man) an opera singer in Berlin. The bus travels backwards. The view of the trees does not depend on the direction of time. A woman shouts four times (from the fourth time to the first), "Saaid." When the driver removes his head from the engine, something breaks down. An old Arab (his back to the bus, facing Abu-Gosh*) gets on and everyone travels until Bernhard sees fat Alfonso on the other side of the glass.

*A village near Jerusalem

The head of Benbenishti

99

THE HEAD OF BENBENISHTI (SEVENTH generation in Palestine) is being pecked by crows. If he were not busy chasing away the crows (Eyner fun zayneh tatns tates hot mistome opgeshrokn a vorone)* Benbenishti would press Elvira's body to his vest (to his breastplate) and lead her in a tango (which he would use for another purpose). Who will Elvira dance with? Anyone who says she didn't come to Palestine to dance, may his name be cursed. And may his name be cursed if he says anything else. Gustav is out of the running and Bernhard sits on the fence (he is indecisive). If no one dances with Elvira (and holds her body close) in April, dreadful, terrible things will happen.

*One of his forefathers apparently frightened a crow (Yiddish)

D.S. Gregory's love

D.S. GREGORY'S LOVE FOR ISABELLA IS buried deep inside him and that is why it's difficult to think about. But you can ponder the external envelope of the body. D.S. Gregory has resolved to devote his whole life to dermatology (in days to come he will make a habit of saying: "you mustn't belittle sweat and fingernails"). D.S. Gregory speaks naturally and Yekaterina also speaks in appropriate fashion. Nevertheless, matters can be presented as if they were two characters in a book:

Yekaterina was leaning on the pillows, dressed in a red robe.

—Mother, Dear, D.S. Gregory said, I have a request. . . .

Yekaterina spread out her arms.

—Come, she said, and first kiss your mother on her poor cheek.

D.S. Gregory hugged Yekaterina's shoulders and kissed her on both cheeks. A warm vapor arose from her body.

—Now tell me, my son, Yekaterina said, what is your request?

—Mother, Dear, D.S. Gregory said again, Your generous permission to travel to Paris.

—To Paris? Yekaterina asked, and what will you do there?

—I wish, D.S. Gergory said, to study under Professor Casanova.

—Really, Yekaterina said in anger, you're just like your father.

—No, Mother, D.S. Gergory said, you are mistaken. Professor Casanova is a well-known expert in the field of dermatology.

—Dermatology? said Yekaterina.

—The study of skin diseases, D.S. Gregory explained.

—Yekaterina's eyes widened in astonishment.

—Skin diseases? she cried. Are you out of your mind?

—No, Mother, D.S. Gergory said, I have given the matter a good deal of thought. I have decided to devote my life to the study of the skin, and there is no better place anywhere in the world than le Hôpital de St. Louis in Paris. Beside Professor Casanova, there are well-known scholars there like Alibert, Biet, and Devergie. . . .

—Devergie. . . , Yekaterina interrupted, Devergie. . . I seem to have heard the sound of that name before. . . .

In short, in Paris

(IN SHORT, IN PARIS, D.S. GREGORY RENTS a modest bachelor apartment on Boulevard Saint-Michel, not far from the hospital. On his writing desk, next to the book by Bonomeau, he places the portrait of Isabella, etc., etc. . . .) He discovers, to his surprise, that the ancients (Aristotle, Celsus, and Galen) had already studied diseases of the skin, but that they believed diseases of the skin, like internal illnesses, are caused by a disruption in the balance of bodily humors. In the 16th century the well-known French doctor Jean Togault produced a detailed description of skin diseases in six volumes. And Bonomeau, in 1868, discovered, for the first time in the history of dermatology, an external cause for skin diseases (the scabies tick, *Sarcoptes scabiei*). In Vienna, in 1776, Jozef Plenk proposed a system for the definition and classification of skin diseases, based on symptoms that appear on the skin. But D.S. Gregory's teachers, Casanova and Alibert, hold that Jozef Plenk committed a gross error, and one should accept the classification system of the Englishman, Robert Willan (with reservations on some details). They ridicule Antoine Lorry, a follower of Jozef Plenk's system, and hate him fiercely.

Dogs are howling

DOGS ARE HOWLING AND WHIMPERING— a sign that the Angel of Death is abroad in the city. But if a man leaves his house in the morning and from the opposite direction a dog comes up and plays (i.e., cavorts and prostrates itself in front of him), this is a sign that all will be well. Oy, today Elvira Neuwirth will sip a glass of schnapps with Bernhard (in Gustav Benjamin's house). Gustav will put a record of Johann Strauss on the Gramophone and Elvira will start to dance,

Ta-Ra-Ra-Ra-Ram   Pam-Pam   Pam-Pam
Ta-Ra-Ra-Ra-Ram   Pam-Pam   Pam-Pam
Ta-Ra-Ra-Ra-Ram   Pam-Pam   Pam-Pam
Ta-Ra-Ra-Ra-Ram   Pam-Pam   Pam-Pam

Happy Birthday! Elvira's body (all its protuberances and orifices) passes, in April, from one year to another. And, although her fingers move only in the major key (she doesn't have fantasies at times not set aside for that purpose), she needs some great festivity.

At ten, approximately

AT TEN, APPROXIMATELY, ELVIRA WILL BE
tipsy. She will laugh to herself and press Bernhard to
call her "Elvira" (she'll think: "So what? So what?").
Within the whirl (in the place where there is no
movement) the sharp pain will cut through Bernhard's stomach. Gustav will suddenly disappear.
But at the same time (or a moment later) Bernhard
will dance in front of Elvira as if nothing had happened, and Gustav will stand by the Gramophone.
And when the moon enters the window frame, Gustav will say "eins, zwei, drei, vier" and the two of
them (Gustav and Bernhard) will say together
"Mendele drank kefir."

In May, the English bomb

In May, the English bomb the Ruhr and Eider dams. The water breaches the stone embankments and floods the open plains. Iceland declares her independence from Denmark (she rises above the surface of the ocean and says: "I am not dependent on Denmark"). They kill Krüger, chief of the Gestapo in Poland. First he scrubbed his armpits (a place that is usually neglected). He had clipped his toenails before getting into the bath. Between his (Krüger's) body and the bottom of the tub there was a narrow space the size of a snake (but if they had put a snake in there, its lungs would have filled up with water). Krüger's thought (i.e., the thought that Krüger thought) before they killed him was: "Ich bin Krüger."

On every thorn barb

ON EVERY THORN BARB THERE HANG
(early in the morning) drops of dew. Butterflies, almost unreal, flutter towards Jericho. If Herzog were
not scrupulous in observing the commandment to
wash one's hands (with lots of water and all the
other details) he couldn't earn a living. When Herzog meets Bernhard, he pulls a button on his vest
and tells a story of two gentiles and a Jew. But in
Bernhard's May imaginings, Elvira is unlike the
Elvira of April (her voice is coarser and the dance
more frenzied). If Benbenishti danced with Elvira,
he would press her breasts, as it were quite naturally, to the fine English cloth he bought in Beirut
(Benbenishti's male organ is his own flesh and
blood). And since Bernhard's soul is on the loose,
Herzog says: "I advise you, Mr. Stein, every day
you should say Psalm 38, which is a powerful spell
for finding a mate. And if you cannot say the whole
Psalm, then say out loud, and with great devotion,
the passage: 'Lord, all my desire is before Thee: and
my groaning is not hid from Thee.'"

The good Lord places into Elvira's hands

THE GOOD LORD PLACES IN ELVIRA'S HANDS a long thin metal shaft (she interweaves woolen threads). In her dreams mirrors shatter. And why, damn it, aren't there flowers on her head? Everyone is preoccupied with other matters. Let Lord Halifax and Leslie Hore-Belisha put a garland on her head. Let Ben-Gurion put a garland on Elvira's head. Let Rabbi Uzziel put a garland of flowers on Elvira's head. Palestine has become abhorrent to her (mosquitoes bite her flesh). She needs a telephone! Let lines stretch beyond her house. Let an accountant (born in Lithuania but educated in Vienna) invite her to the Atara café for coffee with cream, and apfelstrudel. She will lean her arm on the table and Mr. Weinfeld (or Mr. Kurz) will say: "And there is a second office. . . ."

In 1825 a German doctor

Like cures like.
(*Latin*)

IN 1825 A GERMAN DOCTOR WHOSE NAME was Friedrich Hahnemann came to Paris and said: "Similia similibus curantur."* Friedrich Hahnemann performed experiments on his own and other people's bodies, and came to the conclusion that the cure for an illness is found within the illness itself. Man (the German said) exists by virtue of his inside, and not as generally supposed. Psychic influences (found in invisible particles of air) feed the body fluids. Friedrich Hahnemann's speech is strange and his face fat. But the skin is really only an external crust. One thing touches another and the air moves about like the waves of the ocean. Sounds fill the empty space, yet the ears (which stick out from both sides of the skull) capture only the tiniest amount.

The doctrine of Friedrich Hahnemann

108

THE DOCTRINE OF FRIEDRICH HAHNEMANN
(that there is a kind of spirituality in the air) is accepted mainly by women of the aristocracy. At
times, when answering a question, he forgets that he
ought to say "Oui" and says "Ja." "It cannot be
said," he says, "that the 'anima' (soul, spirit, psy-
che) is found in one place and not in another. Fol-
lowers of materialism believe that matter is solid as
iron and lifeless as a lump of clay. But even in a
stone there is a rustle of life. There is no corner in
the whole universe without movement, and the
source of that movement is not something external
to matter, but matter itself."

The Materialists

THE MATERIALISTS MAKE FUN OF HIM. "This anima," they say, "that the German believes is found in the body, is it a kind of insect? Does it have senses of its own? Does it have two pairs of wings and three pairs of legs and two antennae and two eyes? And when the German dies, will it break through the flesh and come out on his skin? And where will it go from there, the miserable little creature?" Friedrich Hahnemann says: "They can say what they like. There are more things in heaven and earth than are dreamt of in their philosophy." But at night, on the other side of the wall, he hears the sound of the chopping of salad greens (the tapping of a knife on a block of wood). Someone calls out "Bernadette" or "Bernhard" and then there is silence.

                                            Bernhard thinks

BERNHARD THINKS: "THIS SPIRITUALITY (i.e., the spirituality of Friedrich Hahnemann), is it spiritual or not spiritual? If (he thinks) the spirituality of Friedrich Hahnemann is spiritual, then it is the spiritual spirituality of Friedrich Hahnemann. But if (he thinks) the spirituality of Friedrich Hahnemann is not spiritual, then it is the unspiritual spirituality of Friedrich Hahnemann. One way or another, both of them (i.e., the spiritual spirituality of Friedrich Hahnemann and the unspiritual spirituality of Friedrich Hahnemann), derive from Friedrich Hahnemann's spirituality. And while this spirituality is a first principle, it can still be broken up into different categories among which there are only the slightest of differences.

Gustav (for instance) knows

GUSTAV (FOR INSTANCE) KNOWS THAT HE grew up in an orphanage in Nordeney in Germany, and came from there, by ship, to Palestine. But he does not know who his father and mother were. One may ask: Does the Divine Presence rest upon Gustav? If the Divine Presence rests upon all mankind, then surely it also rests upon Gustav. But in his whole life Gustav has never heard of the Divine Presence. Could it be that it (i.e., the Divine Presence) rests upon Gustav without Gustav knowing that it rests upon him? If they tell Gustav (in Hebrew) that the Divine Presence rests upon him, he will ask the tellers to tell him in German. And how could they tell him, Gustav, that the Divine Presence rests upon him, in German?

In June, Sidney Cohen lands

In June, Sidney Cohen lands on the island of Lampedusa in the Straits of Sicily because of a mechanical fault in his airplane. The garrison on the island raises a white flag and Sidney Cohen, on his own, accepts their surrender. The air is full of smells. Bernhard thinks: "Could there possibly exist a man called Mischkulinski?" or "An Indian house is called a wigwam." The world is big and wide (it is filled with facts—for instance, that Fraulein Schmidt did not understand that in the end everyone dies, and that she herself is now dead). To avoid error one must speak clearly and to the point (first things first and last things last): how a man was born, how he grew up, how he studied, how he thought, and how he died.

It is very difficult to arrange

IT IS VERY DIFFICULT TO ARRANGE EVENTS in their proper order. Shereshevsky (the grocer) became ill and they operated on his heart. They cut into Shereshevsky's white chest and peered at his flesh until his heart was revealed. Herzog flies by virtue of his small prayer-shawl. His kneecaps knock together. He buys (at the pharmacy) a little camphorated oil, soaks a wad of cotton wool in it and then puts the cotton wool, once every day, in his ear. Bernhard says, "Excuse me" in a German accent. His neck is wrinkled (especially at the back). His feet are odd. Crows stare at him with one eye, and then turn their head and stare with the other eye. (His body is transparent. Rays of light break up inside it and divide into colors).

When one looks at fat Alfonso

WHEN ONE LOOKS AT FAT ALFONSO FROM the outside, it is impossible to see what's inside. But in the hollow of Alfonso's stomach are the liver and the gall bladder and the spleen and the small intestine and the large intestine and the urinary canal. And God also created Bernhard in His image (in the image of God, He created him). God's face is Bernhard's face, and Bernhard's face is God's face. The spirit of Bernhard moves upon the face of the waters (without form and void; and darkness is upon the face of the deep), but someone shouts "zol zayn likht"* and afterwards, as in a kind of nightmare, the waters are gathered together in one place, and the dry land appears.

Let there be light (Yiddish)

And Gustav too

And Gustav too will work wonders. He will stand on Mount Scopus (or some other mountain) and someone will come and say "Achen!"* And when Gustav thinks about Aachen, which is in the Rhine Valley, Palestine will lose heart. Bernhard thinks: "One should die in the winter. The sounds will slowly fade away and everything will cease without pain." If a woman called Hilde had known Bernhard, she would have called him by name. No one knows the power of a single word (like, for example, "Etwas"†). Sometimes it is hard not to be sentimental. When you love people like Bernhard or Gustav, tears flow by themselves. One day they will all be dead, and someone else will talk about other people. But even if he were like the person who is talking now, and the people he talks about are just like Bernhard and Gustav, he will still be a different person and the people he talks about will not be Bernhard and Gustav, but other people.

In September, Englishmen

*Surely! (Hebrew)

†Something (German)

IN SEPTEMBER, ENGLISHMEN AND AMERICANS land on the beaches of Italy. Their woolen socks are soaked in water. Germans and Poles kill Jews wherever they find them (also in September). In October, the Danes smuggle out their Jews to Sweden. (That strange and ugly child, Hans Christian Andersen, who everyone mocked, was in the whole world loved only by his grandmother. Only she took him to her heart with gnarled hands. His bent grandmother. And that is why little Hans Andersen saw fairytales. Just because of her. Just for her. And she alone shall reign upon earth, by the decisive power of her loving kindness, which smells of cheese and old age.) On the sea between Copenhagen and Malmö, the literary critic Georg Jacobsen says to himself: "When all this is over, I shall write an autobiographical memoir, and call it 'Georg Jacobsen's Jammersminde.'"* Mrs. Weiss (who is sailing on a different boat) asks: "And when your son comes of age, what will he do?" And the fisherman says: "Holger is not an exceptional student. He will fish with me, and after I'm gone, he will inherit the boat and the nets."

*"The Chronicles of the Sufferings of Georg Jacobsen" (Danish)

In February, the Germans

IN FEBRUARY, THE GERMANS SHOOT THE Armenian poet, Misek Manushian. Shimon Finkel*

raises one leg in a kind of dance and says: "Take it easy Golde, don't lose your temper! Don't moan, my love, and don't be downcast. This is a day of joy. We have good fortune coming." And Golde says: "Good fortune? Misfortune and misery! Have you already lost the red cow? Did you sell her to Lazer Wolf for a pittance?" (It's impossible to know what Gustav is thinking. His head is not made of glass. But if he had travelled to Tel Aviv, by bus, to see "Tevye the Dairyman," he would almost certainly have remembered the fable of the brave tailor who killed seven flies with one blow.) "I did even worse!" says Shimon Finkel and Golde says: "Did you trade her for another, a finer cow? Did you outsmart poor Lazer Wolf?" "Worse than that, my angel," says Shimon Finkel and Golde says: "So come to the point, and I'll listen! You and your talk—every word costs a fortune!" "Congratulations, Golde! Congratulations to both of us! Our Tzeitel is getting engaged today!" Shimon Finkel says and Gustav (who was created in the image of Primordial Man, with

†*What happened? (German)*

light flowing from his mouth, his nose, and his eyes), if he had been there, would have bent his head and whispered in Bernhard's ear: "Was ist passiert?"†

In 1920, when Bernhard's father

IN 1920, WHEN BERNHARD'S FATHER DIED, the window was half open. A large bird entered (from outside in) picked up the nightcap and left (from inside out) and flew over the roofs of Berlin, and everyone saw the bird and the nightcap and said: "There's a bird, and there's a nightcap, and there's the name Sigmund Stein which his mother embroidered, when Sigmund was a boy, in red thread."

That hour was, certainly, the hour of the bird. The nightcap slid over the window sill and the bird soared up into the sky. You may think: "Sigmund's nightcap is in the sky over Berlin." And you may think: "Sigmund's nightcap is in the sky over Bernhard's head." But you may also think that the sky of Berlin is, at all times, over Bernhard's head, so Sigmund's nightcap is in the sky of Berlin over Bernhard's head, in Palestine. There are secrets that no one knows about like, for instance, when we sleep Flemish peasants that Brueghel painted rise out of the mouth. And there is a secret that people forget all the time. Sometimes they remember it's there, but forget what it is, and sometimes they even forget it's there.

One must understand

ONE MUST UNDERSTAND EXACTLY WHAT is happening. Bernhard (and not someone else, or just anybody) is sitting in Palestine in the heavy, black coat of his father, Sigmund. One must also understand what is meant by "Bernhard thinks." The room on Prophets Street is similar to the room Van Gogh painted. On the shelf stand the works of Schiller and the works of Goethe and the works of Heine, and Schopenhauer and Nietzsche, and Wilhelm Busch and twenty-one volumes of the Brockhaus Encyclopedia and the "History of the World" (published by Ullstein), and the "Complete German-Hebrew Dictionary" of M.D. Gross (sole distributor, Benjamin Hertz, Berlin-Wien). But the skies of Palestine swirl among the pine trees, round and round, and blood drips from Bernhard's ears.

Awake, he sees terrible sights

AWAKE, HE SEES TERRIBLE SIGHTS. DEATH has already come out of hiding (like petals) in Shereshevsky's body, but his wife is plucking feathers. She sticks her hand into the chicken's stomach (she is careful of the gall bladder), takes out the innards, puts them in a pot (she also adds carrots and parsley, covers the table with a lace tablecloth, picks up the soup ladle and serves from the pot into two plates. (He thinks: "A man dies just like an elephant. All at once. The great body collapses and the earth trembles. Letters . . . and smells . . . and possessions. . .")

In April, Elvira makes

In April, Elvira makes the acquaintance of Major Slocomb. He says and she says and he says and she says (on King George Street children sing "Do Re Mi Fa Sol / Hitler tarnegol").*

*Hitler is a rooster (Hebrew)

Major Slocomb says: "What is 'tarnegol'?"
And Elvira says: "A Hahn†".
He says: "A Hahn?"
And Elvira says: "Na, a Henne‡".
He says: "A hen?"
And Elvira says: "Ja, but a man-hen A Hahn."

†Rooster (German)

‡Hen (German)

In his imagination Bernhard pictures Major Slocomb and his mother in England. Major Slocomb sticks his finger in the jam jar and his mother (with protruding teeth and receding chin) whispers "Christopher!" Major Slocomb pulls his finger out but sticks it in again, and his mother whispers "Christopher" over and over again until Bernhard no longer knows whether Major Slocomb's mother whispers "Christopher" because he sticks his finger in the jar, or whether he sticks his finger in the jar because his mother whispers "Christopher."

He thinks: "It says

HE THINKS: "IT SAYS IN THE *Shulkhan Aruch** that you mustn't think about holy matters when on the toilet seat. But if Herzog heard the sound of his hair he would know that the entire world is the body of Herzog, and every seat is a seat of glory. Birds would fly directly towards his face. Indescribable odors would arise from his body. 'My Herzog,' a young woman would say, 'those leather straps that you wind around your arm. . .' And, afterwards (in an entirely different photo album) he would relive his childhood. Chasing a butterfly and the butterfly flies away. Chasing and the butterfly flies away."

*The Prepared Table, *a book in Hebrew by Joseph Caro* (1488–1575), *is a major compendium of Jewish religious and legal practices.*

In June, a great and powerful army

IN JUNE, A GREAT AND POWERFUL ARMY crosses the English Channel and breaks through to Normandy. Benbenishti hears about Sigmund Freud. His teaching (so Benbenishti says) is based on the assumption that man's life is motivated by wishes hidden in the "unconscious" and desires repressed into the "subconscious." Psychic disturbances (Benbenishti says) have their source in these hidden desires and therefore man is called upon (he says) to understand what is going on in his soul, so that he may know how to marshal his actions and his words.

The Red Army captures

THE RED ARMY CAPTURES THE EXTERMINATION camp of Maidanek. Sunrays break up in the warm air, and the shape of things trembles and blurs as if seen through a flame. Things happen (as, for example, a peddler cries out "Pfirsiche"*). Looking from top to bottom one first sees empty space. Then there is a crate of peaches. Then you see the body of the donkey (his spine and his stomach) and his male organ. Below this are the paving stones. However, you can refute the peddler's words by hurrying up and saying (before he cries out "Pfirsiche"), "Nicht."†

*Peaches (German)

†Not so (German)

In Berlin, when he was still a child

In Berlin, when he was still a child, Bernhard saw (he remembers) Old Kovacs on the cinema screen. Old Kovacs stood on the railway line, his hands thrown forward, and his fingers spread out. The train came closer and closer, but Kovacs didn't blink an eyelid. Only the tip of his moustache trembled in the light of the head lamps. Since then Bernhard has known greater sorrow (Sigmund died and Clara died) but the death of Old Kovacs who stood alone, at night, and tried to stop the train by the power of his gaze alone, was the first.

The world, Bernhard thinks

THE WORLD, BERNHARD THINKS, COMES
and goes. Old Kovacs has to summon up all his
spiritual power in order to stop the train. The locomotive engineer steps down and the two of them
(the engineer and Kovacs) sip brandy. Kovacs says:
"It was nothing. I just concentrate." The locomotive engineer says: "My father also knew how to
hypnotize. But not trains." (Kellermann's fat father
hypnotized stars. He used to say: "You have to
know how to look from afar.") And Kovacs says:
"My father was a simple carpenter. But my mother
was a spiritual woman" (Kovacs' mother was a
spiritual woman).

Kellermann's paternal grandfather

KELLERMANN'S PATERNAL GRANDFATHER
was born in the Hungarian village of Kis-Kor. He
was the fireman (he held the coal bucket in both
hands: the fire lit up half his face) and when he lay
on his death bed (very thin and clean) he said: "All
my life I dreamt you would become. . . How do
you say it?" and the fat boy (Kellermann's father)
said: "A locomotive engineer." The fireman died.
Black hair grew on the widow's face. The street children (there was no street in Kis-Kor) called her and
Kellermann's father "Fatso and the Bearded Lady."
Kellermann's father prayed to God to remove the
beard from his mother's face (he said: "Please God,
don't let my mother have a beard"). At night he lay
on his back in the clover field of Mendel Grubi (a
poor Jewish farmer) and stared at the sky and
thought: "Those points that are up there are. . .
are. . ." (his forte was not thinking).

The moon rose

THE MOON ROSE AND MENDEL GRUBI
(his smell remained in the wooden bed) awoke for
midnight prayers.* First he cried over the destruc-
tion of the Temple and the exile of the Divine Presence. Then he strode round and round his clover
field (when the wind blew, his prayer-shawl flapped
like deformed wings) and recited, in a subdued
voice, verses from the Psalms and the Book of
Lamentations. Kellermann's father (at that time he
wasn't his father since Kellermann had not yet been
born) lay there, in the grass, and saw with his fleshy
eyes how the ancient letters left Mendel Grubi's
mouth and rose (from the clover field in Kis-Kor) to
the stars.

*Prayers for the
restoration of the
Temple*

Mendel Grubi finished his prayers

MENDEL GRUBI FINISHED HIS PRAYERS
and went back home and the fat boy (Kellermann's
father) remained in the field alone. A million stars
shone in the sky. A white mist rose from the grass.
And then. . . how can such a thing be explained?
(In days to come Kellermann's father would say:
"The moon and the stars went mad.") When the
boy's eyes moved left, the vault of heaven also
moved left. And when his eyes moved right, all the
hosts of heaven moved right, in one solid block (exactly at the rate of movement of his eyes).

Kovacs' mother was abandoned

KOVACS' MOTHER WAS ABANDONED BY gypsies at Novi-Sad, seven parasangs from Kis-Kor, on a blacksmith's doorway. Adam Horvath (a poet: he wrote the poem, "Oh, she shall give me such a wild soul, that I shall sail like a gypsy o'er the plains of Hungary, my native land") said to his wife (the widow of another poet): "If we take the manuscripts of Imre out of the attic, we can put the girl up there" and his wife said: "Poor Imre. There was something about his writing that was bright (i.e., sun-drenched) and full of hope."

And since the girl

AND SINCE THE GIRL (KOVACS' MOTHER)
had never heard Hungarian, Adam Horvath
pointed to his house and said "haz." And when
Kovacs' mother understood that "haz" means
"house," Adam Horvath taught her the proper way
to pronounce "hazban" ("inside the house"). After
this he pointed to the root of his nose, moved his
head closer to hers and said "latlak" ("I see you").
Kovacs' mother laughed and said "latlak" and
Adam Horvath also said "latlak" and laughed.

In Novi-Sad, from now on

IN NOVI-SAD, FROM NOW ON, THEY WILL tell (amid fumes of alcohol) weird and wonderful stories. The notary Dohnanyi will say: "It has long ago been proven that a man's character is hereditary. If the father was a gypsy, the daughter will be a gypsy as well." And Arpad Jozsef (a lyrical drunkard) will say: "Constantinople! (a cry of wonder commonly heard from the inhabitants of Novi-Sad). They say that at night a rat sleeps in her lap and on the window sill, on the other side of the glass, stand. . . Constantinople! . . . birds without necks."

At night the girl

At night the girl (Kovacs' mother) thrust a finger and, in the swamps around Novi-Sad, frogs croaked. Adam Horvath said: "In the interaction between body and soul it is difficult to know for certain which is the effect and which is the cause. But, as a rule, it's better to assume the superiority of the spiritual. There is undoubtedly something spiritual in the air, like electricity." His wife said: "Imre would say that what you don't achieve by hard work, you don't achieve at all." Adam Horvath said: "That is evident in his verse." His wife said: "What do you mean?" Adam Horvath said: "I mean that Imre was hard-working." His wife said: "You can't say he wasn't" and fell asleep. Adam Horvath picked up a goose feather dipped it into the ink and wrote down, with one stroke of the quill:

> Let us all bow down
> To that Primordial Being
> Who moves all mankind around
> From naught to existence
> And vice-versa.

In August, Shereshevsky, the grocer

IN AUGUST, SHERESHEVSKY, THE GROCER, dies. The grocery is locked and early in the morning Bernhard goes to the grocery on Zunz Street and asks for a bottle of kefir. He has a strange dream. In his dream his mother Clara has a dream, and in her dream a mummy which is kept inside a glass case in a museum in London is about to disintegrate. In those days telephone wires did not yet stretch from Berlin to London, and Clara travels, first by train to Calais in France and from there, by ship, in order to save the mummy. And on the ship, between Calais and Dover, in the heart of the English Channel, Bernhard is born. But on some political pretext hidden from the dream, a German doctor with great force pulls the body of Bernhard out of the body of Clara. A lanky warrior from Afghanistan takes pity on Clara and stands by her (at times his back is covered with red clay, to ensure courage), a lance in one hand, until she arrives in London. In the second half of the dream, Bernhard himself (on his forehead a scar that the German doctor left) comes to London and sees that the mummy that Clara had seen in her dream is still lying in the glass case, its legs tucked into its stomach. On the wall of the museum there is a kind of gauge that measures the dryness of the air, and Bernhard looks at the gauge that his mother Clara had looked at before and sees that it is made from lots of springs, and on the wooden box is written, in gold letters, 1902.

Towards the end of September

TOWARDS THE END OF SEPTEMBER THE Americans reach the outskirts of Aachen. Gustav lies (because of a stomach illness) in "Misgav Ladach,"* and Bernhard goes there every day (but because "Dach" is "roof" in German, and the Hebrew for roof is "gag," he says absent-mindedly "Misgav Lagag") in the afternoon and sits with Gustav for two whole hours. On the intermediate days of the Feast of Tabernacles Gustav pulls up his trousers and goes home and there, in the kitchen, he lets a teaspoon fall and drops of tea splash the glass plate on top of the table. Between the table and glass there are all kinds of payment vouchers and receipts, and Gustav can see (you can't know what Gustav can see but when you look in his eyes, you can see where he is looking) that the letters under the drops are enlarged beyond their proper size.

In the middle of the night Bernhard says: "Let's imagine someone selling hats. He shouts 'Hüte! Hüte!'† but no one believes him." Gustav says: "Are the hats visible?" and Bernhard says: "The hats are visible."

He thinks: "There are times

*A hospital in Jerusalem

†Hats (German)

136

HE THINKS: "THERE ARE TIMES WHEN LIFE is very bitter, and a man lies down at night and cries, and in the morning his eyes are red and everyone can see he has been crying, and they tell him to go and talk to a psychologist, who is well-versed in the study of the mind. And he goes to the psychologist and talks to him and at night the psychologist, who has his own sorrow, lies between the sheets and cries." "And this," he thinks, "is a kind of vicious circle, with no way out except some decisive act (i.e., once and for all) like, for example, a woman with breasts, and dark nipples in the middle of them that drip milk, placing the offspring of a different mammal on her stomach, and the baby licks the milk and does not die."

Feldmarschall Rommel commits suicide

FELDMARSCHALL ROMMEL COMMITS SUICIDE
and following him Generalfeldmarschall von Kluger
and Generals Wagner and von Taraschkow also
commit suicide. Field Marshal Lord Gort, the new
High Commissioner, comes to Palestine. At noon,
when the sun is shining, Herzog says: "Kinderlakh,
shpilt zikh nisht oifn gas."* But after evening
prayers he goes out under the sky, fragrant and
dressed in fine clothes, and says the blessing for the
new moon. At first, he determines if its rising can be
seen on the ground (as written in the *Shulkhan
Aruch*, and if it's covered by a cloud, he doesn't say
a blessing unless the cloud is thin and unsubstantial). And in the middle of the blessing, the moon
(half of it already blessed) looks at him and says:
"Kinder, lakht! Shpilt zikh oifn gas"† and Lilith,‡
the long-haired whore, comes to him and se-
duces him and becomes pregnant with the seed he
spills.

Herbst in Jerusalem

*Children, don't
play in the street.
(Yiddish)*

†*Children, laugh!
Play in the street
(Yiddish)*

‡*Female figure in
Jewish folklore*

HERBST IN JERUSALEM.* BERNHARD PRESSES his finger to his eyeball and things become doubled. (Gustav leaves his body and stands beside himself. Over the head of the first Gustav hangs an electric bulb, and another bulb, whose light is paler, hangs over the head of the second Gustav.) The word "Irkutsk" fills his heart with joy. He thinks: "Some-one should write the history of legs (i.e., the history of their behavior throughout the ages). The book on Elvira's legs would be called 'Die Füsse von Elvira Neuwirth'† and would have four chapters." And he also thinks: "Herzog's face is covered with pim-ples. He says 'Vos' instead of 'Vas' and if they said 'Got hot a zun'‡ he would collapse. But his legs are very important (Herzog's legs are very important)."

*Autumn in Jerusalem (German)

†"Elvira Neuwirth's Legs" (German)

‡God has a son (Yiddish)

He draws an imaginary line

HE DRAWS AN IMAGINARY LINE FROM THE crown of the head of the fat child from Kis-Kor (Kellermann's father) to the stars, and from there (i.e., from the stars) another line to Adam Horvath's attic in Novi-Sad. Both lines become (because of the great distance between Hungary and the sky) one line. And though from the highest place all things are equal, below in Kis-Kor itself, things are distinguished with absolute clarity. The street children run after the fat child (Kellermann's father) and his widowed mother. One of them bangs a tin drum and the others sing in chorus:

In Kis-Kor ("my little garden") / On a lovely Spring evening / Aunt Rosa rides a goat / She pulls its tail / The apples fall / And Aunt Rosa, joyfully, eats to her heart's content.

Kiskertemben szep tavaszi esten, esten
Rozsi neni lovagol a kecsken, kecsken
Meghuzza a farkat
Potyognak az almak
Rozsi neni vigan falatoz.*

When the moon is

WHEN THE MOON IS IN THE EARTH'S half-shadow, the fat child (Kellermann's father) leaves his widowed mother's house and walks seven leagues (all the time his heart is going Pom-Pom Pom-Pom) from Kis-Kor to the outskirts of Novi-Sad. And there without knowing why, he circles Adam Horvath's house six or seven times. Adam Horvath is fast asleep (his face towards the ceiling) on the ground floor, but upstairs, in the attic, the blood of the girl (Kovacs' mother) is overflowing. Her womb can no longer contain all that blood, and the blood spills out from between her legs onto the sheets.

And when there is a full eclipse

AND WHEN THERE IS A FULL ECLIPSE OF the moon, Mendel Grubi goes out to his clover field and performs a great ritual of redemption. First he blows broken notes on the ram's horn, according to the number of the breaks in his body (one broken note for each break). The broken sounds that leave his mouth in a minor key blend with the music that is constantly played (like a music box) by the stars. And since the danger arises that the music of the seven spheres will be discordant (all of it is in a major key), organs join the celestial choir. When Mendel Grubi realizes that the upper sounds are about to overcome the lower sounds, he goes to the church (bats flit around the prayer hall), pierces his feet with an old nail and pours blood into the metal pipes from which the sounds emerge.

The girl conceived

THE GIRL CONCEIVED AND EVERYONE
thought Adam Horvath was the father. The notary,
Dohnanyi, puffed on his pipe and said: "Anyone
who lies once will lie again." But Arpad Jozsef (a
lyrical drunkard) stood up, flushed with anger, and
declared: "Anyone who says that Adam Horvath
stuck it in, may his name be blotted out. This is not
the first time this has happened. The child is holy
and his mother is a virgin." Adam Horvath shut
himself up in his house and wrote his famous poem
"Oh, Heaven Be My Witness."

> Oh, Heaven be my witness!
> I am a mass of bruises.
> I am hurt all over
> With fresh blows.
> People surround me
> Like a pack of wolves.
> Only two know
> That my heart is pure:
> I myself, and God.

And while he was writing

AND WHILE HE WAS WRITING, HIS WIFE (Imre's widow) went, her feet swollen, to the house of Kovacs the carpenter, and pulled the bell. Kovacs the carpenter had already gone to bed, but when he heard the sound of the bell he sat up (his toes hardly touched the wooden floor) and shouted in Hungarian: "What?" Adam Horvath's wife shouted (also in Hungarian): "Open the door. I want to ask you something, sir," but Kovacs, the carpenter, shouted a second time: "What?" Adam Horvath's wife knelt in front of the door and shouted into the key hole: "Does the gentleman, that is to say you, want to marry the girl?" Kovacs the carpenter said "Good" and put his feet back under the blanket.

When the baby

WHEN THE BABY (I.E., OLD KOVACS) CAME
into the world, Adam Horvath wrote his poem
"Demons Pointed Their Fingers":

> Demons pointed their fingers
> And said "Thus!"
> And I said, "There has never been
> Any such thing."
> My heart is as pure as a blue
> Sky on a summer's day.
> And if I am found guilty
> In the court of this world,
> In the court
> Of the next world
> I shall be innocent.

When they came to tell Kovacs the carpenter the
baby had been born, his head was bent over a half-
finished stool. They said "It has happened." He said
"What?" They said "She has given birth." He said
"What?" They said "A boy." He said "Good," and
picked up his lathe.

In January, the Red Army captures

IN JANUARY, THE RED ARMY CAPTURES
Auschwitz. Water freezes in the pipes. Gustav boils
water in a kettle and pours it on the pipes, and a
white mist rises and spreads in the air of the room.
Bernhard looks at the large mains which bring the
water from under the ground to the pipes inside
the house, and sees they were made in England, in
the city of Manchester. He imagines the sights once
seen by the makers of the mains (copper pipes, air
bubbles in a glass of beer, red walls), some of them
already dead and some extremely old.

People, he thinks

PEOPLE, HE THINKS, TAKE PHOTOGRAPHS of views and hand the pictures to each other and say "Here's the mountain" or "The second from the left is Joachim." But you have to understand how, when Elvira reaches for the tea caddy, things really happen. Over Elvira's head hangs an electric bulb (when King Boris the Third of Bulgaria died, his wife Giovanna cried until the tears wet the collar of her dress). Elvira's fingers touch the tea caddy. Light surrounds her body. The world only appears solid, but actually the elements keep reverting to heat.

Old sights spring up

O<small>LD</small> <small>SIGHTS</small> <small>SPRING</small> <small>UP</small> <small>IN</small> <small>HIS</small> <small>MIND</small>. H<small>IS</small>
mother Clara, her body thin fabric, in a dark cor-
ridor, and outside in the light of the sun, a German.
Clara says, "kommen Sie bitte Mittwoch"* and the
German nods his head. A young woman (her eyes
inversely blue) grips his shoulders. Her lips move
but her voice is inaudible because of the great distance. "And this sight too. . . ," he thinks to himself, "Good, dear Gustav holding a teapot. . . ,
this sight too, is already only a sight in the
memory." A sharp pain cuts through his stomach
and at that very instant Gustav vanishes for a moment and reappears. But he knows that these things
happen, not in the real world and not in the world of
fantasy, but in another world.

*Come, please,
on Wednesday
(German)*

On the thirteenth

ON THE THIRTEENTH, THE FOURTEENTH, and the fifteenth of February the Allies bomb Dresden. Sixty thousand Germans die. On the twenty-sixth of February, one thousand two hundred American warplanes drop three thousand tons of bombs on Berlin. On the fourteenth of March, five thousand warplanes drop bombs, each of which weighs eleven tons. And on the twenty-first of March, at the Spring Equinox, seven thousand warplanes drop bombs, whose total weight is twelve thousand tons.

In April, Mussolini

IN APRIL, MUSSOLINI AND HIS MISTRESS Clara Petacci are killed. Hitler poisons himself. Bernhard and Gustav go to the Atara (Gustav waves his hands as if the world were filled with water and that's why he must grab an oar) and there, in the Atara, Bernhard imagines to himself that he (i.e., Bernhard) suddenly gets to his feet and announces to everyone that the sound bees make is called "Buzzing" and everyone is astonished. He wants to bring evidence from a book, but everyone insists that such evidence is worthless, since he wrote the book himself. But when he asks what they all think the sound of bees is called, they all cover their private parts with their hands and blush.

V-Day. Everyone goes

V-Day. Everyone goes out into the street and makes the V-for-victory sign. But out of humility, Bernhard does not stretch his arm up like everyone else, but holds his hand in front of his face. He tries with all his might to separate his forefinger from his third finger, as is proper, but his fingers draw together and the victory sign doesn't come off well. He sees signs of the coming redemption. A large crow, almost as big as a penguin, hops in the street and shows no fear. Water leaks from a bucket of sewage and stands like glass pipes in space. "In a little while," he thinks, "Old Kovacs will slide down Prophets Street on a harp. He'll lean the harp against the wall of Rappaport's shop and say 'Jonapot.' Afterwards he'll say 'hogy van' and finally 'nevem Kovacs' and everyone will go to the Atara and drink coffee with cream and eat apfelstrudel."

On King George Street

ON KING GEORGE STREET, IN THE HEART of the crowd, a young woman hangs on his neck and presses her lips to his face. "For six years," Bernhard thinks, "the whole world has turned upside down for this purpose." Suddenly he remembers that Paula said before she died "Muschl, what will you do alone?" And he (i.e., Bernhard) said: "you mustn't talk like that." He imagines his soul ascending (a kind of circle of light) to Heaven and meeting Paula's soul there. Paula's soul welcomes him and says: "Komm, Muschl, I've been waiting a long time" and both souls (Bernhard's and Paula's) float off together and greet other souls.

In June, King Haakon the Seventh

IN JUNE, KING HAAKON THE SEVENTH OF Norway, returns after five years of exile to his palace in Oslo and cannot find his pipe cleaner. Everything is covered with dust. He searches the long corridors for the palace housekeeper, but Amalie Garborg died of pneumonia in 1943 (how many years have passed, Haakon thinks to himself, since anyone in the world called me "Karl"). He goes to the library and takes down *Creation, Man, and Messiah* by Wergeland* and reads that the Messiah is "the hope of the people, the terror of kings and priests." In the end he finds his pipe cleaner in the bedroom and uses it to scratch between his toes.

*Henrik Wergeland (1808–45), poet and Norwegian nationalist leader

On the sixth of August

ON THE SIXTH OF AUGUST THE AMERICANS drop an atomic bomb on Hiroshima, and on the ninth of August they also drop a similar bomb on Nagasaki. In the cinema Bernhard and Gustav see the dust cloud that rises from the ground where previously there had been a Japanese city, and climbs higher and higher in the sky, and they say almost in unison: "Wie ein Riesenpilz."* On the second of September on the deck of battleship *Missouri* the Japanese sign the instrument of surrender. President Truman says: "America will not forget Pearl Harbor, and Japan (he says) will not forget the *Missouri*. . . ." "So many things," Bernhard thinks, "the heart forgets."

*Like a giant mushroom (German)

If he were a character

IF HE WERE A CHARACTER IN A NOVEL (and not flesh and blood) Bernhard would go to the house on Strauss Street and see that the weeds in the courtyard have already reached the height of a man, and he would stand by the gate and remember things that happened there (like Paula once going out onto the balcony, or the wooden shutter being displaced). In reality, he goes to the Dung Gate and an Arab, with a face like Benbenishti, pulls at his sleeve and says, "You want woman?" Bernhard wants to educate the Arab and teach him that in English the noun must be preceded by "a," but he is afraid the Arab will think him (i.e., Bernhard) talkative because his soul craves intimacy, so he just says "yes."

Ay, ay, either redemption

AY, AY, EITHER REDEMPTION IS AT HAND or Bernhard is about to find himself in a brothel. And since redemption is not at hand, Bernhard is about (by virtue of this syllogism) to find himself in a brothel. Think nothing of it. Strict observers allow prostitutes for ordinary Jews and forbid them to priests, but Maimonides permits them for everybody. Pope Innocent the Third conferred sanctity on every man who went with a prostitute and in Toulouse in France, the proceeds from the brothels were divided between the municipality and the university (the town hall employees and the professors came to the prostitutes with the prostitutes' own money). And the Emperor Justinian outdid all of them when he became infatuated with the ankles of a certain Theodora and made her Empress of Byzantium.

The Arab walks through

THE ARAB WALKS THROUGH THE VEGETABLE
market and Bernhard walks behind him. Bernhard
has an erection. His thoughts revolve around
Descartes' philosophy: God created mind and matter, and they move separately, each in its own path,
and are matched like two clocks made by a master
craftsman. When one clock shows the hour, the
other clock chimes. When the soul desires something it is like the first clock which shows the hour,
and when the hand reaches for the object that the
soul desired it is like the second clock that chimes
according to the hands of the first clock. The soul
cannot move since it is not in space, and the body
cannot think since it is not mind, but God created
them like those two clocks where one never goes
faster than the other, and since that act of Creation,
the world moves of its own accord like clocks with
wound springs, and God need not intervene again,
and He sits in the heavens and observes His cre-
ations from there.

The Arab walks up

THE ARAB WALKS UP SIX STEPS AND RAPS
on an iron gate, and the face of a woman appears in
the space between his face and the frame. He says
something in Arabic and the woman turns her head
to Bernhard and speaks in Greek, and Bernhard sees
that her body is long like a butterfly's and that she is
heavy with child. He wants to run away, but the
woman's voice is like his mother Clara's. "My
mother, Clara," he thinks, "is transparent as a vase.
Her breathing is clear, but within her stomach a
small body of blood is being formed (you can see,
through the glass, how the heart is beating). The
body of blood feeds on itself and continues to ex-
pand until the glass body can no longer withstand
the pressure and shatters." And when he comes in
her, the tip of his body seems to touch the child inside her stomach and push it gently, as you push a
child sitting on a swing in the park, and the child
screams and is afraid and begs "Higher" and
"Harder" until the swing is about to overturn.

In October, the French condemn

IN OCTOBER, THE FRENCH CONDEMN TO death Pierre Laval who was Prime Minister. Pierre Laval poisons himself, but they manage to revive him and execute him according to law. Bernhard imagines Pierre Laval opening his eyes and seeing sheets and a white ceiling. At last, Pierre Laval thinks, it's all over. The prison doctor comes and stands by his side, and Pierre Laval is surprised that things happen as in the other world (only somewhat transparent, he thinks, and unsubstantial). And when they tell Pierre Laval "Vous allez mourir comme meme,"* he realizes that every world has its own death. The dead man dreams he is alive, and dies in his dream.

*Nevertheless, you will die. (French)

On Ibn Shafrut Street an old man stops Bernhard and looks at him through a convex lens. "Sind sie nicht," he says, "der Sohn von Sigmund Stein aus Berlin?"† But when Bernhard goes to the place the old man mentioned and rings the bell, an old woman opens the door and says "Herbert died yesterday."

†Aren't you the son of Sigmund Stein from Berlin? (German)

The word "Marheshvan"

THE WORD "MARHESHVAN"* PLEASES
Bernhard. He thinks: "Good morning, Mr. Hesh-
van! Do you think Mr. First Rain will be so kind as
to fall from heaven today?" He takes a handful of
sand in his cupped hands and lets it trickle between
his fingers until the ant lion which was inside the
sand remains alone on his hand. The gray insect
feigns death and lies there motionless. But when
it realizes that passivity will not save its life, it
squeezes its body between the hands and pushes its
way through the folds of the skin. Bernhard digs a
little hole with the heel of his shoe and places the
ant lion inside. The ant lion lies for a long time at
the bottom of the hole and can hardly believe its
good luck. Suddenly, it throws grains of sand every
which way, and is swallowed up by the earth.

Richard Byrd sets out

*The second month of
the Jewish calendar;
"Mar" is, in
Hebrew, also
"Mister."

RICHARD BYRD SETS OUT ON HIS LAST voyage to the Antarctic continent. Richard Byrd will see things that no man has ever seen before. But even he will not see the heart of the continent, a place hidden by clouds and storms, between the Weddell Sea and the Sea of Ross. In 1914 Shackleton and Macintosh tried to reach there. Shackleton sailed on the Weddell Sea and Macintosh on the Sea of Ross. Both ships became trapped in the ice. Macintosh's ship floated with the ice for 315 days until it managed to break free and return to the sea from which it started. Shackleton's ship was crushed by the ice and the crew floated 457 days on an iceberg until the iceberg broke apart.

The shores of Antarctica

THE SHORES OF ANTARCTICA ARE COVERED, along their entire length, by a layer of ice that merges with the ice covering the sea. It is impossible to determine its size. From the surface ice that covers Antarctica mountains of ice break off and float on the sea. To sailors they look like islands and are listed on the maps and given names, and only later does it become clear to the sailors who come after them that these islands do not exist.

The peaks of the mountains rise to over 6,000 meters but because of the layer of snow and ice, no one knows their true shape. Immense icebergs break off from the mountains in the center of Antarctica and slide hundreds of kilometers down the frozen valleys until they reach the icy walls that encircle the continent and slip into the ocean. At the heart of the continent the temperature drops to 80 degrees below zero. The winds blow at great speed. Columns of snow rise to heights of hundreds of meters, and it's impossible to distinguish between snow falling violently from the clouds and snow rising, driven by the wind from the ground.

On the second of January

ON THE SECOND OF JANUARY, KING ZOG
of Albania is deposed. In his mind's eye, Bernhard
sees all the ministers arrive in silk robes and bow before Zog. Zog sits up straight on his throne, the Albanian crown on his head, and says: "We wish you
and your wives. . . ." One of the ministers cuts
him short. He makes an obscene gesture with his
hand and says: "Achmed, move!" Achmed Zogu
cannot believe his ears. He continues as if nothing
has happened: "Happy New Year! And we wish to
add. . . ." The minister spits out a gobbet of yellow tobacco onto the marble floor of the palace and
repeats: "Achmed, move!" In order to hide his em-
barrassment, the king quotes from the ancient epic
of Albania *Kenge Kreshnikesh,* the verse "Ancient
snows had fallen there / Its head was crowned with
clouds." The national author, Mjeda, has pointed
out that this verse only appears to describe Mount
Korab (whose peak rises to a height of 2,750 meters). In reality, the poet hints at the royal house of
Albania, whose authority derives from Heaven. But
the minister had not read the works of Mjeda, which
is why he says, for the third time: "Achmed, move!"

On the tenth of March

ON THE TENTH OF MARCH (FOUR YEARS
before he declares that the Virgin Mary ascended to
Heaven) the "Holy See" grants an interview to Yitshak Isaac Ha-Levi Herzog, the Chief Rabbi of
Palestine. Already, as a young man, Pius the
Twelfth had carried the papal pelvis from Rome to
Bavaria. Now he raises both arms (Yitshak Isaac
thinks: "Oykh mir a khokhem"*) as if in great
mercy. Tongues of flame shoot forth from the fire-
place. "If the opening for the smoke (which is called
'roykhfang')," Yitshak Isaac thinks, "is at the side,
so that the blockage is like an additional partition,
then plugging it is permissible. But if it is above, it
is forbidden, since it is like the Tabernacle, to plug it
on the Sabbath." Crafty Pius twists his lips in a thin
smile.

*Another wise guy
(Yiddish)

In April, Elvira sails

IN APRIL, ELVIRA SAILS WITH MAJOR
Slocomb to the town of Cockermouth in the Lake
District. Bernhard imagines Elvira (surrounded by
grassy meadows) leaning on a stone, the northern
half of which is covered with moss. "Ach," she says,
"William Wordsworth . . ." And the Major says:

> Why, William, on that old grey stone
> Thus for the length of half a day,
> Why, William, sit you thus alone,
> And dream your time away?

"And there's another poem," Elvira says, "about
Narzissen."* "Narzissen?" says Major Slocomb,
and Elvira says: "Na, the flower in the Sumpf."†

*Narcissi (German)

†Swamp (German)

Things happen

THINGS HAPPEN WHICH ARE VERY DIFFICULT to explain by logic. A chameleon wraps its tail round a branch of a tree on Prophets Street. One of its eyes looks backwards and the other forwards. In the morning its body is greeny-grey, but in the afternoon the colors change to greeny-blue with brown spots. Gustav goes to the market and buys a chicken and puts it into a basin in the bathroom. The chicken stretches its neck and looks at the corners between the walls (but not at the walls between the corners). Finally, it disentangles itself from the string that the Arab had tied around its legs and plunges to the floor. And when Bernhard sees nothing left in the basin but three feathers, he is reminded of a thick-set woman who once stood on Abarbanel Street and shouted "Moise!"

In May, Vittorio Emmanuel the Third

In May, Vittorio Emmanuel the
Third, King of Italy, abdicates in favor of his son,
Umberto, and goes into exile. But after twenty-
three days Italy becomes a republic, and Umberto
the Second follows his father into exile. In Tel Aviv
Shimon Finkel throws out his right hand and recites
in a loud voice:

> . . . Why thy canonized bones, hearsed in
>   death,
> Have burst their cerements. Why the
>   sepulchre,
> Wherein we saw thee quietly inurned,
> Hath oped his ponderous and marble jaws,
> To cast thee up again. What may this mean
> That thou, dead corse, again in complete steel
> Revisit'st thus the glimpses of the moon. . . .

And when the Ghost answers him and says: "I
am thy father's spirit, / Doom'd for a certain term to
walk the night. . . ," Bernhard thinks: "Oh, Sigmund!" and his heart is wrenched from its place.

Forgotten sights arise

FORGOTTEN SIGHTS ARISE IN HIS MEMORY.
He once took down Sigmund's nightcap (it smelt of
Sigmund) and stuck his head into it. And when Sigmund said "Here's Clara," he asked, "And the bag
too?" and Sigmund said, "The bag too." "And the
owl too?" and Sigmund said, "The owl too." Then
he peered out from the nightcap and his mother
Clara's face really stood there in the room, and the
yellow bag was under her arm. Clara took the felt
owl out of the yellow bag and placed it on his stomach, and he hugged the owl with both hands and
thought to himself that Clara also took out little
Bernhard—Abracadabra!—from inside the yellow
bag, nightcap on his head.

During the interval

DURING THE INTERVAL BETWEEN THE THIRD
and fourth acts Bernhard and Gustav go out into the
lobby of the "Ha-Bimah" theatre and Gustav
drinks soda water and says (in German) "How
beautiful Ophelia is." And when the gravediggers
lower Ophelia's body into the grave and her brother
Laertes says, "Lay her i' th' earth, And from her fair
and unpolluted flesh / May violets spring!" Bernhard thinks: "Where is that ray of light that in 1925,
in Hamburg, stretched from the curtain and
touched the hair of Anne Marie's head? Now a different Anne Marie lies there and a ray of light (rays
of light were not twisted by the blast of the bomb-
ings) extends from the curtain to the opposite wall
and a different Bernhard puts his hand on the ray of
light and his flesh lights up and his bones become
visible (as then) inside the flesh."

In the last scene

In the last scene the Queen dies and
the King dies and Hamlet dies. Fortinbras enters
with drum and colors, and Horatio says,

> But since, so jump upon this bloody question,
> You from the Polack wars, and you from
> England,
> Are here arrived, give order that these bodies
> High on a stage be placed to the view. . . .

And after all this they carry the bodies off and
everyone leaves and the stage remains empty (and
from a distance the sound of cannons is heard).
"And if," Bernhard thinks, "there is another world
after this world, the nights in that world (like a pho-
tographic negative) will be white nights and a ray of
black light will touch the flesh of the dead."

In July, an explosion

IN JULY, AN EXPLOSION BRINGS DOWN the King David Hotel on its occupants. The English arrest fat Alfonso, and his mother (her face is seen through the window) holds, between her thumb and index finger, a blue marble she had placed in the cradle when Alfonso was born (the tissues stretched until the sides of the womb were about to tear, and suddenly the soft, wet body, slipped out) and recites a spell said in times of danger. And when they tell him, Alfonso, at the police station, "Hurry up!" he remembers, by some kind of hidden association, the odor of apricots he once smelled in the vegetable market in Izmir.

Bernhard has dreams

BERNHARD HAS DREAMS. OSIP BOVE KNOCKS down the wall surrounding Zemlyanoy Gorod and in its place paves a broad avenue. But instead of lying flat on the ground, the avenue winds up like a roll of cloth. Yekaterina sips tea with blackberry jam. Her thoughts are hollow. She looks at the sky framed in the window and grasps the secret of formlessness. "Pavel is gone," she says, "and gone too is his leg that never was." Another dream: an oil painting by Oskar Kokoschka. Under the painting is written "Benbenishti's legs" and someone says, "Oskar was mainly successful in painting the veins."

The Autumn Equinox

THE AUTUMN EQUINOX. NATURAL EXISTENCE
achieves equilibrium. Bernhard sits in Gustav's
house, in the kitchen. Gustav prepares tea under the
electric bulb, and Bernhard listens to the St. John
Passion by Johann Sebastian Bach. His thoughts
carry him to Mrs. Knoller (who lay with two com-
panies of soldiers near Stalingrad). He sees her in
her room in Bucharest. In her hands, which are almost transparent, are fortune-telling cards. She has
become very beautiful. Within her soul the last
dams have been breached. And looking for her are
Dimitri Minulescu and Jon Giorgescu and Negulici
the cook (who carved women dolls from wood) and
all the rest. He writes letters:

Department of Philosophy. The University.
Mount Scopus. Professor Doctor Franz Levin.
Thank you for your letter in which you ask for
information about the philosopher Ludwig
Stein who died in 1930. Unfortunately, I am
not a relative of this important philosopher. If
my memory does not deceive me, my father
(Sigmund Stein, who died in 1920) told me
once that Ludwig Stein, although living in
Berlin at the end of the 19th century, had his
origins in Hungary, while my father's family
came to Germany from Holland, probably already by the 17th century. I first became acquainted with the writings of Ludwig Stein in
the early 1920's when I was a student of Philosophy at the University of Berlin. At that

time I read in the journal *Archiv für Systematis-che Philosophie* that Ludwig Stein was its editor. Later on I came across his book *Die Soziale Frage im Lichte der Philosophie,* and I remember being very impressed with the way Ludwig Stein explained Immanuel Kant's theory of knowledge and with his very deep optimism, which all of us seemed to share in those years.

Magda Moser, Bismarckstrasse 13, Section VIII Berlin. Dear Magda, this is the fifth letter I have sent you. I sent the first before the war, and I do not know if it reached you. The other three letters that I sent at the beginning of the war were returned because postal connections with Germany were cut. I hope with all my heart that this letter reaches you, though I suppose you are no longer living in your old house in Berlin.

Oh Magda! Your sister Paula, my dear wife, died on the 18th of September in 1938. Eight years have passed since then, but the grief is still great. At first, Paula became increasingly thin. Afterwards, black spots appeared on her legs, back and stomach, and from June onwards, she did not leave her bed. On the 17th of September Paula fell asleep a little after ten in the evening. At three-thirty in the morning when I awoke from sleep, her eyes were closed and her face at peace. But her breath had ceased.

Dear Magda! We have never met, but I know you well from Paula's stories, and I do not want to entertain the possibility that you were injured during the war. I know you did not agree with Paula's Zionism, but Paula did not regret coming to Palestine (even though she suffered from the heat and the mosquitoes) and I believe she was happy in the last years of her life. I imagine you will no longer wish to live in Germany, and I would like to remind you that the house that Paula bought with your family's money legally belongs to you. No one lives there now. The house has three rooms and is located on a quiet street, with a yard surrounding it, and in the yard there are eight pine trees (*Pinus halepnesis*), which are somewhat different from the kind of pine (*Pinus silvestris*) found in Germany.

And when the Crucified Jesus looks at his mother, the Virgin Mary, and says, "Behold, woman, here is your son" (and the chorus sings, "Behold now the Righteous One / In His final hour") Bernhard gives birth to a child, and Gustav stands suspended in space above the rooftops of Jerusalem.

—The End—